HOME TRUTHS

For Mum. Thanks for bringing me home.

HOME TRUTHS

MYTH DUSTING BY THE LADY OF THE HOUSE

MANDY NOLAN

FINCH PUBLISHING
SYDNEY

Home Truths: Myth dusting by the lady of the house

First published in 2015 in Australia and New Zealand by Finch Publishing Pty Limited, ABN 49 057 285 248, Suite 2207, 4 Daydream Street, Warriewood, NSW, 2102, Australia.

15   8 7 6 5 4 3 2 1

There is a National Library of Australia Cataloguing-in-Publication entry available at the National Library.

Edited by Samantha Miles
Editorial assistance by Megan English
Text typeset by Meg Dunworth
Cover design by Ingrid Kwong
Printed by Griffin Press

Finch titles can be viewed and purchased at **www.finch.com.au**

CONTENTS

INTRODUCTION   1
1   Home, sweet home   6
2   Bless this share house   24
3   Feng Shite   36
4   The long way home   44
5   The people in your street   59
6   Home alone   67
7   I wash, therefore I am   76
8   The house that Jack (and Jill) built   87
9   Almost home   104
10 Beige, sweet beige   118
11 Homework   125
12 In the comfort zone   138
13 The haunted house   147
14 The joy of socks   159
15 A room of her own   162
16 The beep test   174
17 The pet project   181
18 Toilet talk   192
19 Love thy neighbours   201
20 Finding home   208

No woman gets an orgasm
from shining the kitchen floor.

Betty Friedan

(Really? Maybe she is not doing it right.)

INTRODUCTION

*T*here's something strangely melancholic about revisiting places you once knew as a child. Everything seems so much smaller, or stiller, and it's always much less impressive. Places that seemed magical in childhood have their mundaneness revealed in adulthood. *On the way to one family holiday,* I remember talking up the Big Banana to my kids. I delivered a soliloquy about how massive it was and how visiting it was just this awesomely unforgettable experience. As it turned out, my family's reaction to the Big Banana led one of the kids to nickname it the Big Disappointment. And they were right. It wasn't even that big. My four-year-old daughter was so devastated by the banana's inability to deliver on the excitement I'd promised that she sat in the car and wept, managing a 'I hate the Big Banana,' between sobs. Maybe our kids aren't as easily impressed as we once were. I guess we are the dinosaurs from the pre-digital age – kids these days are more impressed by how small things can get. I didn't dare stop at the Big Pineapple.

The nostaligic memory that makes things bigger, better and so much more impressive than they actually were is one of the true beauties of childhood. Our infantile perception and lack of experience allows us to construct much more elaborate stories then the ones that actually existed.

A few years ago I took my kids back to the country town where I grew up, to visit my dying grandmother. Although I had visited the town intermittently over the last few decades, it was on this trip that I finally realised that the place of my birth wasn't a bustling country town alive with commerce and cheery folk but, in fact, a hot, dry and dusty streetscape of quiet desolation. The place looked nothing like the town I grew up in. The town that I remember was quaint, pretty and green. Fast forward thirty years and the place I saw from the window of my seven-seater people mover was bleak. My kids were appalled. One of them gasped in horror, 'You grew up here? Oh my god, I'd rather die.'

I made the mistake of telling this story in my regular newspaper column, where I used a less fancy word than desolate. It might have been 'shithole'. Of course, I never meant to offend people still living in the shithole. In fact, it never occurred to me that the shithole residents would ever read the article that referred to their beloved town as a shithole. I write for a regional newspaper about 700 kilometres south of the shithole. I thought my story was only being told to people who lived outside the shithole. Who would have thought that shithole citizens would have the internet? (Maybe it's not such a shithole after all ...)

I discovered that I'd extended my regular reach with my weekly rant when my mother rang. She left the shithole years before but still had regular contact with a few friends left clinging to the bowl. 'What have you done?' she exclaimed. 'Your brother and I have had people ringing us all week!'

I later discovered that someone had found my story about the shithole online and told someone who told someone else, who emailed it to someone else, who printed it out and letterbox dropped it. Opening my hole had landed me pretty well up to my neck in, you guessed it, shit.

I opened my Facebook page and found numerous messages, including one very charming one from a girl I went to school with that read, 'Mandy Nolan you fucking mole you should be ashammed of yourself for what you said.' While I generally make a point of not commenting on comments, particularly when they are abusive, I couldn't resist correcting her spelling. Let's just say she wasn't the brightest light on the porch. Another woman sent me a long and very cruel message accusing me of neglecting my grandmother. She went on to say that my grandmother wouldn't know who my children were but that she knew her children by name because they visited her regularly. Of course she didn't say it as eloquently as this: hers was more along the lines of 'Mandy Nolan you is a cunt.'

Like most people who are attacked by angry mobs, I couldn't see what I'd done to incite their ire. I'd written what I considered to be a humorous and, at times, touching article. My homecoming had been sad and I wanted to relate some of that sentiment to the reader. I had drawn a parallel between the decline of my grandmother Ivy, a 94-year-old powerful and fierce matriarch, and the decline of her and my beloved town. It was picked up and printed in the local paper. It was talked about on the local radio. People wrote letters to the editor. A family friend rang me personally to warn me I shouldn't come home for a while. 'You were a bit harsh Mandy,' she said. 'You called it a shithole. You could have at least called it … a shit box.' Point taken.

Eventually I was invited on air to discuss my article on the shithole with the mayor. This was three weeks post-publication date, and my 800-word article was still making the rounds. The mayor was a pleasant enough chap and actually told me that since my article, defensive citizens had rallied to defend their town, and even an 85-year-old woman had joined Facebook to be part of a group called 'I love Wondai'. That is the name of the town. I wasn't going to mention it, in case I got a second wave attack of hate mail when the book goes viral. Then I thought that would be good because it meant that they would be buying the book. The only downside is the shithole I come from is too small to make much of an impact on sales. If only I'd been born in a big shithole. Somewhere like Ipswich, then I'd be pumping some serious digits.

The mayor and I chatted quite amiably once we'd worked through the shithole comments and I'd tried to contextualise it by telling him it was less of a criticism and more of a metaphor. Then of course I had to explain what a metaphor was. 'It's not meant to be insulting,' I explained. 'I just used the image of the withering decay and decline of the town as a parallel for my grandmother's infirm state.' I don't think he liked my metaphor. I guess when you own real estate in a shithole, you don't want smartarse fly-by-nighters like me going public with the news that the place is a shithole. In the end the mayor actually thanked me for helping kickstart what was turning out to be a passionate and quite well organised campaign to reinvigorate town spirit.

Guess the residents of the shithole where I grew up owe me an apology …

Three months after the furor of the shithole comment faded my grandmother died. After the initial grief and the tears for the loss of a woman who had such a profound affect on who I am, I suddenly realised I would have to go home. Oh dear. Shithole, here I come. A person really should learn to watch what she says, because shit has a habit of not only hitting the fan but sticking where it lands.

This is a book about home – about who we are in the place where we live, how we live, where we live, and what we become in the process. I don't think I can tell a story of home without taking you back to where I come from. So strap yourself in and make sure you bring some repellant – for insects, rednecks and me.

This is my home truth.

HOME SWEET HOME

Home is where one starts from.

T.S. Eliot

Welcome to Wondai, the place that coffee forgot. Going home shouldn't give you a migraine, but that's what lay in wait for me every time I returned to visit my mum in the sleepy home town where I grew up. Caffeine withdrawal is a bitch. By the third day the headache was so bad I actually contemplated snorting a line of Pablo off Mum's kitchen bench top.

Coffee came to Queensland late, and good coffee even later. I now know why. Country Queenslanders are not coffee-drinking people. Since I'd left home, I'd become a soft inner-city dweller used to strong lattes made by weak vegetarians or swarthy Italians. Here, in the country, people drank tea. In fact, I think it would be true to say that in Wondai the awfulness of the coffee was in direct relationship to the greatness of a cup of tea.

No-one makes a cup of tea like country folk. And none of this Twinings Earl Grey, English Breakfast dingle your bag up and down nonsense. That's sacrilege. It's as offensive to a hard-core tea addict as a tin of international roast is to a coffee lover. Good tea is made from leaves, usually Bushels or Billy Tea, and brewed in a metal teapot, covered in a garish crocheted cosy and poured into a well-stained china tea cup with precision in spite of the arthritic tremor. I didn't appreciate this until later when I became a 'tea person'. During most of my life I would identify myself as a 'coffee' person. It's like the beverage version of knowing your sexual persuasion. Although I knew people who drank tea, and I sometimes liked a cup of tea myself, for many years it was coffee that hit my B spot!

In the early years you couldn't get a good coffee in Wondai. Not at home. Not at the shops. At home, coffee came from a tin. I could mark the evolution of our social status with our instant coffee brand upgrades. We were a family who'd started out Pablo, followed shortly by International Roast and then by the time I was in my mid teens we were on Moccona Gold. The little jar was so impressive you didn't put it in the cupboard. No, you left it on the bench so that other people knew that you were on the way to becoming upper working class. Hell, you might even be lower lower middle. Affluence was just a few jars away. I still remember how proud I was when I had a friend over from school and she marveled. 'Wow, your family drinks Moccona.'

I wasn't always a coffee snob. When I was a kid I loved instant. I think I was about 11 when I first started joining Mum in a bonding cuppa. I started out with one a day (milk, two sugars), and by the time I was 16 I was smashing about eight cups a day.

My favourite coffee was the one I had at bedtime. Then I lay under the chenille spread, clutching the fringe in terror, staring at my glow-in-the-dark Sacred Heart of Jesus painting, having a panic attack, waiting to die. It was freaky the way they'd managed to paint Jesus' heart so that it kind of hovered in the dark air of my room, pierced by the crown of thorns. Children with anxiety conditions should not have violently graphic religious iconography in their bedrooms. Or drink large quantities of caffeine at bedtime.

You couldn't get a 'cuppacinno' anywhere in town. If you wanted something as posh as coffee with chocolate sprinkled on top you had to Kingaroy, or travel another hour to Toowoomba. I don't know why good coffee never came to my region. I put it down to an undersupply of Italians, Arabs and Lebanese and the oversupply of white Anglo Saxons.

There is one thing I've learnt: where large groups of whiteys abound, so does pretty average food and even more average thinking. Australia owes its food choices to the eradication of the white Australia Policy. I'm dead against this 'Stop the Boats' business. The more boats come into this country, the better our food gets. I'm all for getting rid of detention centres and installing Masterchef kitchens and universities. Multiculturalism broadens the palette and the mind. And damn it if they don't make some kick-arse coffee as a bonus. I think it would also be true to say that our children have got a lot better looking with all the cross-cultural interbreeding. We've suddenly got chins, smaller ears, our eyes have moved apart, our noses have shrunk and we finally have necks. So Tony, please, for the sake of our genetic, intellectual and culinary futures, let the boats in.

I was home on one of my visit-the-family-at-Wondai-sojourns (this usually preceded cornering my mother and asking her for money), when I popped down to the local café to get some hot chips. You'd think hot chips would be a country town specialty but unfortunately, oil changing was more of a centenary event than a weekly one. That's when I saw her – a giant shiny stainless steel beauty. La San Marco, the first and only Italian in town. She was beautiful. A state of the art coffee machine, the one embraced and loved by the most demanding espresso addicts in the world. I could scarcely speak. Coffee had come to Wondai. Maybe it was time to come home.

'Can I have a cappuccino?'

The waitress kept chewing her gum while muttering, 'Yup'. She then proceeded to take the gum out out and stick it on the glowing body of the machine, before removing the filter basket. Her hand moved towards a jar of Nescafe, which she opened and then filled the basket with it. I couldn't believe it. Where were the freshly ground beans?

She used a $6000 machine to make me a 10-cent coffee. She also hadn't managed to nail the milk-frothing component of the machine so while she managed to make the milk hot, it certainly wasn't fluffy. I swear to this day she was making the frothing noise with her mouth.

'Here's your cuppacinno,' she mumbled as she pushed it across the counter and re-installed the gum. As I sat in the booth drinking my expensive Nescafe, I pondered that the only barista who would come to this town would be the kind that defended cattle rustlers, illegal gun ownership and angry women who turned tables over in cafes that promised cappuccinos but delivered disappointment.

My hometown of Wondai is nestled between Murgon and Kingaroy in Queensland's South Burnett, about 240 kilometres north west of Brisbane. It is not a pretentious place. It is not a beautiful place. It can be at times, but generally it's a hard place, full of snakes and bees and angry emus. Last time I took the kids there they got chased by an emu and bitten on the arse by a swarm of wild bees. It's not the welcome a person expects. Wondai is not an affluent area full of country estates. It is a modest little town full of battlers. Or as I have previously callously described, a bit of a shithole.

So when I was a snotty university student and people asked where I came from and they misheard it as Bondi, I let them. I was a wanker ashamed of my roots. Bondi always seemed so much more fabulous than Wondai – it re-defined me as an inner city surfie chick, not a small town hick, which is what I really am.

I am sure many people have experienced a similar embarrassment about their home town. A deep knowing that no matter how well educated, world travelled or academically lauded you become, you are still a redneck girl from nowhere. Queen of Shitsville.

I still have a fondness for where I come from, although I doubt I'll ever be welcomed back. I think your relationship with where you were born is very significant. Mine is conflicted. I spent my whole childhood waiting to grow up and leave. I worked hard at school, I didn't get pregnant and thanks to the legacy of the Whitlam Government and that tiny window of free education, this daughter of a country town widow scrambled out and got to leave home at 16 and go to university. In the city. Woo hoo. (For some reason Queensland was missing a year of education. Perhaps that's the reason I suck at maths?)

Because of this constant yearning to live somewhere better, I never had a sense of 'home'. I never felt a sense of connection with the place where I was born. It must be a wonderful thing to have that security. That solid sense of belonging to a place. To know home. To know that this is where you are meant to be, or where you will always return. Instead I was born with a gypsy's heart and a chronic case of FOMOOLSB (Fear of Missing Out On Living Somewhere Better).

I always felt different to the other people in my home town. To this day I don't know if that's because I was different, or whether my feelings of difference were exactly the same as everyone else's feelings of difference. Meaning, feeling different is the same. I grew up feeling too tall, too loud, too weird, too left wing, too ambitious and too hungry for a life outside the Pablo jar to ever fit in. In a town full of people with a strong sense of belonging, I didn't belong. I guess I have always been an outsider and until I found a town full of outsiders, I had no home. I now live in Mullumbimby, in Northern NSW, an area famed for its counter culture, its soy lattes, and people who don't immunise their children – they just breastfeed until they are 18. This is a town full of black sheep. If you don't fit in here, you'll be fine anywhere else.

That is not to say that growing up in Wondai didn't have a certain charm. In fact, I still credit the crushing effect of the right wing Christian anvil in helping to forge my gay and lesbian, feminist, greenie, leftie, black-fella loving mindset. In essence, I defined myself as an adult woman in direct opposition to the values I'd grown up with. My mother started it. The daughter of a communist and an aetheist she'd learnt how to keep her godless red head down in a country town. There was no warning about stranger danger when she packed me off for my first day of school, instead she warned me in a hushed tone, 'Don't tell anyone how we vote.' Mum, like me, is also a poofta-loving leftie. And that kind of information would be social suicide for the average five-year old trying to get her turn on the swing.

Wondai was Joh Bjelke's electorate. National Party Heartland. People wore National Party issue homosexual-and-Marxist-repelling underpants. Local brides were known to forfeit cutting the cake and opt instead for a big pumpkin scone. Everyone went to church. Even the paedophiles. I went every Sunday. Sometime weekdays. Let's face it, there was not much else on offer in the entertainment department and although the Catholics put the same show on every time, at least it was a chance to wear a nice frock and get out of the house.

For the time we lived in Wondai, Mum was pretty involved in the Catholic church. After my father died tragically in a car accident the Mick's breakaway Hill Song-flavoured, evangelical

Charismatic Renewal group started visiting. Grieving widows are easy to indoctrinate into the fellowship of creepy Christians. And my mum was just 27, on her own with a six-year-old daughter and a baby boy – she was clearly going to open the door to whoever turned up. I kept hoping it would be the Tupperware Lady so I would have the latest and most awesome lunch box or a lettuce spinner so I could pretend Barbie was in the gravitron, but the Charismatic Renewal mob were first over the line. Fortunately this singing-in-tongues and hands-on-healing-acoustic-guitar-singing-lets-all-go-live-with-the-cult-leader phase was short-lived and Mum flew free, straight out of her charismatic cocoon, albeit to the strains of 'And they'll know we are Christians' but at least she left.

A few years after her stint as a hands-on healer Mum became a more conventional and far less kooky Catholic. She was a late convert, and was one of those unusual new Christians who actually read the bible for the deeper messages, rather than the literal translations that encouraged the killing of children to show faith in God, the vilification of homosexuals and that self-gratifying masturbators would go straight to hell. She found that the Bible's messages of social justice and equality were aligned with her own deeper beliefs, and quite fancied a hippy Jesus who hung with hookers and illegal fisherman.

This was the period of my life that I like to call 'The First Pew Years'. The decade when Mum and her two freshly washed children scored front row seats at the Jesus show. I sometimes wonder if I became a comedian because of the microphone envy.

Every week I watched the priest give his sermon and I remember thinking, *Wow, I could do a lot better than that. The guy has an audience and he's just dying up there.* The priest never made sense. It's like he already knew no-one listened so he just waffled on and on. It was always some really random story like Lot's Wife and he'd warn people to follow God's will, lest we be suddenly turned to pillars of salt. Whenever he read that story all I wanted to do was turn around and see if anyone in the congregation had turned to salt. What if the whole back row had been reduced to giant grinders? I'd be halfway through a quick pivot when a new thought would occur: what if I turned to salt? I wonder if women turned to salt, would god gender equalise his threat and turn men to pepper? Were we all just condiments on his table? Then I'd pray for a brain hemorrhage – not a major one, just something small but still very dramatic. This would see me achieve two goals: a) to become the centre of attention and b) to be removed from this miserable attempt at theatre for the soul. It all seemed ludicrous. No-one cared. People still went home and masturbated to pornography, beat their women and sexually abused children. And that was just the clergy.

I am not meaning to be harsh about the place of my birth. Regardless of the prevailing right wing white is right, pooftas can burn in hell and women belong in the kitchen general political persuasion of the average punter, it's also entirely true to say there were some really good people there. People who didn't tolerate bullshit or artifice. It's an attribute of country folk. They call a spade a spade or where I come from, they call it a fucking shovel.

Country people aren't like city people. They will do stuff for you. They'll come over with casseroles when someone's had a death in the family, they'll milk your cows when your wife's in hospital having a baby and if you turn up at the door in the middle of the night with a dead body, they'll grab a shovel and help you dig the hole.

When I tell people where I grew up they generally try to talk it up and say, 'Oh you lived on a farm.' No, I didn't live on a farm. Living on a farm would have given my country life some sort of purpose. I could romanticise farm life. I would have chickens and horses, I'd be drinking milk from the dairy and hand-raising abandoned piglets. No, I lived in the government-supplied asbestos housing and tamed stray cats. We were townies. In theory, the township existed to service the people who ran the farms who fed and clothed the rest of the country. People who lived in town tended to be broke. (Or alcoholic, or old, or some other form of wretched.) I was a widow's daughter, so opportunities to break free of our quarter-acre block were few. From the amount of teenage pregnancies in my cohort of adolescents it was clear you couldn't root your way out either. A teenage pregnancy just doomed you to living with your parents until you were legal and could be married to the bloke who knocked you up. (If not the actual culprit, then at least one stupid enough to be convinced it was him.)

I was the recipient of some pretty decent country spirit when I lived there, which makes my tactless 'shithole' comments all the more heartless. At 14 I was chosen to play basketball for

Queensland. It meant flying to North Queensland for a series of training camps and eventually off to Perth for the national championships. My family could not afford it. It wasn't going to happen. Those endless hours training down at the local outdoor courts with all the local aboriginal kids asking 'Hey Nola? Nola? How come you so big? Ayyyy … Big Nola!' was for nought. Although in later life I did tell a friend this story and managed to reinstate my indigenous monniker of Big Nola.

In the end Jesus saved me. Well, not Jesus directly but a delightful bunch of ladies from the church who banded together and raised money for me. I am talking chook raffles, cent auctions, cake stalls, the works. In the end I was sent to Perth on the back of a lamington … which is ironic considering these days I'm one of those annoying people who tells other people, 'I just can't tolerate gluten.' I also can't tolerate my fellow gluten intolerants. To this day I am still touched by the kindness of the women I would go on in later life to deeply dishonor and offend by calling their beloved hometown a shithole. I'm sure they hoped for a grander outcome for all their efforts, an elite athelete or an Olympian, someone they could put on the Welcome sign as you come into Wondai other than Chad Morgan, Carl Rackerman and Wondai's Mate. (Wondai's Mate was a champion trotter. Even fast animals get good at moving slow in Wondai.)

No, my name will never make it to the Welcome sign.

Wondai means wild dog. When I discovered that it made sense of the wild bitch I was later to become. Wondai is cattle country. Bushland. The kind of country that poets wrote bush ballads about because this was the kind of landscape that could deliver a sunset so beautiful you'd weep and the next day kill a man. This was a harsh place. Hot and dry in summer, bitterly cold in winter and snakes, well, the world's most venomous snakes lay in wake fucking everywhere. While Wondai was only 20 minutes by car to Kingaroy (where I finished my last two years of high school), it missed out on the volcanic lava flow that had delivered the fertile red soils of a crop-growing region, and thus we missed out on navy beans and peanuts and later down the track, olives and wine. I also missed out on being named Miss Peanut Queen at the Kingaroy Show, a crown bestowed on only the girls with the biggest nuts. I always marvelled that in my entire time living there I don't ever remember one person having an anaphylactic reaction to peanuts. I guess either it didn't exist back then or else the nut allergic people simply swelled up and choked to death in the shadow of the giant peanut silos. There should have been a warning on entering the district: 'This town and surrounding districts contain nuts.' There was no 'may' about it.

When I was a kid, the village of Wondai had a thriving country town centre. Two banks, at least two cafes, three pubs, an RSL, an independent supermarket, a chemist, a frock shop, a gift shop, two hairdressers, a Post Office, a garage, a farm machinery agent, an op shop and Boisons – a rural haberdashery-cum-department store. It should have been heritage listed. Boisons still had the same shop front signage from the 1950s, and many of the same mannequins and stock from the era, marked in pounds. The store was legendary. This was a family business run by bachelor brother Mick and spinster sister Beryl until their death. It was a wonderful place full of surprises. In fact, I once found alligator-skin shoes for £7, which Mick converted at the going rate. Back then the Aussie dollar wasn't so strong so they cost me a whopping $14. There were bolts of fabric that my mother had her wedding frock cut from, buttons in vials that my grandmother had used on some of my baby dresses. You could buy hats, shoes, sheets, blankets, shoes, jammies … it was David Jones' hillbilly cousin.

Sadly, multinational conglomerates and super stores like Kmart, Target and Big W have killed these country enterprises. What was most unique about them was the way they operated in sync with a small town economy. You didn't need money to shop at Boisons, you simply went in, bought your supplies and said, 'Book it up on the account please Beryl.' And Beryl would reach under the counter for a giant ledger that recorded debt and neatly write your name against your purchases. Once every quarter you'd settle the bill. This was a business that responded to the cash flow of a country community, knowing that when the crops came in or the cattle were slaughtered that money is plenty, and that during the long months in between the bank account is often a dry and dusty place. No-one would operate a business like that any more. In Wondai you didn't need a credit card to live beyond your means, you just needed the trust of Beryl and Mick Boison. When I discovered Mum had an account at Boisons it was like getting my first credit card. When Mum was at work I'd sneak down on a Saturday morning for my bias binding or my

ric rac (I was a bit of a home sewer) and book it up. Took Mum
months to uncover my Boison's addiction.

At the time of my last visit it was clear the closing of the nearby
abbatoir and the introduction of the big shopping centres in
neighbouring towns had killed some of the town's local economy.
The banks were long gone, as were the cafes, the hairdressers, the
chemist, and Boisons was boarded shut. I sincerely hoped Mick
and Beryl weren't still inside. Of course the pubs were still going
strong, thank god for the alcoholic economy.

But this town no longer looked like the place where I'd grown
up. There was a strange sadness in noticing how much things
change in your absence. As irrational as it may seem, you kind
of expect things to stay like they are in the photograph in your
mind. I expected nothing to change since my leaving. For things
to stay the same. For the place of my childhood to look the same
as the day I left. Kind of like it was waiting for me.

While Wondai and surrounds was a bit of a multicultural
desert in terms of exposure to Italians, Greeks, Chinese,
Lebanese and Arabic communities, it was and still has a strong
indigenous community. Half the kids at my school in Wondai
were indigenous. An indigenous family lived next door. I had an
indigenous sister Shirley, the daughter of a friend of my father's
who spent a good part of her childhood living with us. I had
aboriginal friends, I knew aboriginal people as part of my everyday
life. It was weird when I got to university and some of my new
middle-class white friends doing indigenous studies admitted
they didn't know any aboriginal people. It seemed bizarre to me

that you could grow up in Australia and not have any experience of indigenous communities.

It certainly made school a lot more interesting. I remember very clearly in Year 9 when Peter Mickelo bought a goanna he'd caught and cooked in for his English talk and then we all proceeded to try it. But don't get the idea that people always lived harmoniously. The racial tensions in my hometown were fierce, and it would be true to say that I grew up in an environment that didn't always value indigenous people or treat them very well. Racism was rife. It would be in the very fabric of people's conversation. People thought nothing of naming their black labrador 'nigger' and calling it loudly in the street, or referring women as a 'bunch of black gins'. I was once even called an 'abbo lover' by someone's mother.

Even my grandmother Ivy, who considered herself a very open-minded person, would often say things like, 'For a darkie he's a very nice fella.' I know she meant this in a complimentary way but it always sounded a bit wrong to me. I would have been six when the kids on my school bus saw me walking home with Shirley, and they teased me with, 'You've got a black sister', 'You're part boong.' I then refused to walk on the same side of the street as Shirley. My maternal grandmother Thelma was looking after me at the time and when she found out what I had done she picked up a switch and she whipped me very hard. She told me, 'You don't ever do that to someone. You walk with Shirley, she's part of your family.' I don't believe you should hit children, but I really appreciate what she did. It was a lesson well learned and helped instill a sense of equity in me between black and white. However, it was a belief system that often saw me at odds with teachers, friends and people's parents.

At my Murgon primary school I was appointed by the nuns to be the bus monitor for the trip out to Cherbourg, the mission community nearby, to pick up a busload of kids. The bus driver hated aboriginals. I had to keep the kids under control so that he didn't lose it. This was quite a huge responsibility for a kid who was only 11. It was really a job for the nuns. I guess they were too busy praying for our souls to actually be physically tending them.

There was one incident that I found so upsetting it stayed with me for life. We'd just picked up the kids and as the bus was pulling out this little girl, she wouldn't have been more than five, came running out late. The bus had just started moving off and she was yelling and waving her tiny arms. Her big brown eyes were full of tears and she looked really frightened. I yelled out to the driver, 'Mr Johns, Mr Johns, stop the bus, we missed Daisy.' He wouldn't stop the bus. He drove off and left a little girl crying on her own in the street. I don't know how Daisy dealt with that, I guess that was just a normal day dealing with the white community. I was so distraught. I couldn't stop crying. I wanted to kill the bus driver. I couldn't believe anyone would do that to a little girl. I went up the front and demanded Mr Johns 'Stop this bus'. He ignored me. Then I told him he was a horrible man, that he was mean and I may have called him a bastard. All I know is that I was removed as bus monitor and a nun was installed the next day.

There is always hope. People do change, and when you live in such close quarters, there's often the chance for some sort of reconciliation. Football was always a good opportunity for that, as the young black boys were magnificent on the field and this contradicted the general belief of the average white supremacist that they were good for nothing. They could certainly out run, out kick and out tackle any of the ruddied-skin, large-eared inbred white boys.

There is a story I love which was told to me about a friend's grandmother. Her family were horrified to find out that she'd been broken into by a young aboriginal man a few days before. Maud was tiny, flat out pushing 5 foot. She awoke to the sound of someone entering her home in the early hours of the morning. When she discovered a young man from a nearby aboriginal community, she asked him if he was all right and if he was hungry. And then she cooked him a steak, made a cup of tea and sat talking with him until the sun came up. Kindness can be disarming. Imagine what the world would be like if there was a little more Maud in all of us? That phone call of demand from the tax department might go a little differently. 'I've noted here that you've missed your recent tax installment and I'm ringing to see if everything is okay? Can we pop around and do the dishes? Mind the kids?'

I love women like Maud. She's my role model. I've had a steak in the freezer for years, but to date no-one has broken in. I guess I should keep some tofu on hand because I do live in the vegan belt. That's probably why they don't break in though, they are protein deficient and haven't got the stamina to get over the deck.

So that is Wondai, my hometown. It's the birthplace of my 'there must somewhere better' and wanker intolerant mindset. Ironically this mindset often causes me great conflict as in the search for somewhere better, I have often found 'somewhere better' to be full of wankers.

I don't intend to linger on the literal place of home for this entire book. I do feel though, that the place where we first stood, the house we lived in, the streets we played on, the faces we saw, are integral to establishing our deeper personal foundations. These are the experiences that helped form our sympathies, our passions, our prejudice, our moralities. It was here we first came to understand who people were, and in a sense, offered us our first understanding of who we were, despite or perhaps because of the tiny world where we lived.

As much as I call this place where I grew up a shithole, and as much as I say I never had a sense of belonging to it, there is still a sense of connection. You can't choose your parents. You also can't choose where you grow up.

This place not of my choosing was the foundation stone of me.

Sure, it's a shithole. But it's my shithole.

BLESS THIS SHARE HOUSE

Oh no, the front door's exploded!

Rik, *The Young Ones*, 1982

If *Sex in the City* had shagged *The Young Ones*, then you'd come close to describing my first sharehouse. Five girls with suspect hemlines and even more suspect morality who ended up living together in semi-organised squalor for two years. This share house on the corner of Drake Street in Brisbane's West End was more significant than any of the others that followed because it was formed by an unlikely but perfect combination of characters. Drake Street was the coming together of different strands of emerging womanhood. This wasn't just a share house, it was a rite of passage. A disgusting pigsty, a lady den of inequity, and also the foundation of the most enduring friendships of my life. I love these girls. And now these girls are all women, some of them mothers, some of them not, living everywhere from Mullumbimby to Melbourne, Brisbane to New York.

Welcome to the House of Fun! Our first all-girl share house was the chance to live life in complete defiance to the constraints, conditioning and expectations of our upbringing. This was our chance to be wild, uncompromising and free as we stepped out of the Nice Girl panties of our upbringings. This was the universe's invitation to be truly appalling. Oh god, it was so much fun! I'm surprised I survived. If any of my daughters moved into a house like Drake Street, I'd insist they move immediately.

My mother was the only mother of all the girls who not only visited Drake Street, but actually slept over. On a mattress on the floor. She literally sprayed a ring of cockroach repellent around her, curled up in the foetal position and slept in a face mask and rubber gloves. Knowing my mum has the same obsessive cleaning disorder that I developed in later life, and the same tendency for extreme anxiety and panic, I now realise what an act of love it was for her to visit me in my happily derelict circumstance.

I look back to the girls we once were and smirk. We ended up together partly by accident, partly by design, and now I think about it, it was like a casting agent came in and auditioned roles. It seems too bizarre that we could have come together by serendipity and not design.

There was Jo, the purple-mohawked punk princess who sang in musicals and majored in Women's Studies and Psychology; Di, the fastidious auburn-haired vegetarian, quietly intelligent and organised in the chaos of everyone else's racket; the beautiful Rowena, an ex-hairdresser who ignored the scorn of her feminist flatmates and unashamedly read Mills and Boon and cooked the sunday roast, and the bohemian Donna who performed in community theatre and dreamed of going to Guatemala and participating in a revolution. I don't think it mattered which one. Just as long as she could carry a flag and dress like Jane Fonda in *Klute*. And there was me, a loud-mouthed, bleach blonde viking failing to pass journalism and most of her family's expectations.

In our TV series, we weren't the spoilt, middle-class, designer-clothes wearing thirty-somethings but were instead, make-up free, hairy arm-pitted under 20s in Doc Martens living at least two bread rolls below the gluten-filled breadline. Back in 1985 no-one was gluten intolerant, which was lucky because it's all we ate. Potatoes, pasta and toast. After all there's nothing better than gluten to soak up goon.

Goon was our drink of choice. Mainly because we didn't have a choice. Goon was cheap. For those who have never enjoyed the delights of wine in a box, goon was the street name for cask wine. Liquid crack. You could get 4 litres for $3. That was almost enough to get all of us pissed. We were generally a two-goon household as the goon to girl ratio had to account for the guests. We always had guests. I don't think there was a night when someone didn't sleep over. Sometimes boyfriends. Sometimes girlfriends. Sometimes friends of friends and sometimes out of luck strangers we'd met and invited home to sleep on the couch.

Drake Street was one of those open houses. That wasn't really planned, it was just that we all lost our house keys in the first week so for the next twelve months, entry was via a window on the staircase. If you wanted access to the house you had to perform a break and enter in full view of the street. It must have been a curious sight to view teenage girls trying to get a foothold on the window sill while wearing giant Doc Martens. Docs are not housebreaking shoes. It's hard to get a foothold in a 2-inch rubber sole. I guess none of our parents had given us the lecture about house security and how public B&E sent a strong message about your lack of home security.

After coming home from a gig one night and finding a bloke climbing out the window, we had a house meeting and decided that we should get some more keys cut.

The intruder incident occurred on returning home from seeing Nick Cave and the Bad Seeds at a local Leagues Club. (I know, can you imagine the über cool Cave doing a footy club now?) He was supported by the late Screaming Jay Hawkins, who performed 'I Put a Spell on You' with more than a touch of voodoo. It was quite a gig. The smoke machine was on full bore the entire time. Either that or it was the effect of a large group of university students smoking in the mosh pit. Having your skin pitted with cigarette burns was common in the 80s. Sure it scarred, but it made a great cover for cellulite.

The taxi pulled up and the five of us rolled out onto the pavement, only to catch a glimpse of a male figure emerging out of our personal break in window. We stood and watched, shocked that a stranger had broken in while we were out. The stranger wasn't remotely apologetic. Instead he looked at the bunch of mismatched punk, new romantic and swampy girls and snarled, 'You don't even have tea.' He was right. We hadn't been shopping and the cupboards were bare. It was insulting to be reprimanded by a disgruntled bandit for not having done the shopping. He didn't even apologise. In fact I think he wanted us to apologise to him. 'Not even worth the effort,' he said as he slammed our front gate. I apologised and climbed in the window through which our beverage-seeking bandit had left.

Our house occupied the corner block of Drake Street with a bus stop directly out front. We found the small groups of business people and travellers who gathered at our door weekday mornings very amusing. Often we'd wander out in our jammies with cups of tea for the people who were waiting. (After the break in, I made sure that we always had tea.) We liked flirting with convention and making tea for strangers seemed like a pleasant aberration from the unspoken social norms. Being nice to people who weren't expecting it became one of our sources of fun. Once we all put on 1970's long flowing chiffon dresses, hats and lipstick, made a pavlova and cake and trifle and then walked to the park in a silent procession, holding our sweet treats high in the air. By the time we hit the park we had about three stragglers who'd joined us, and by the time we lay the blankets out for our impromptu community picnic there was a small gathering of faces we'd never seen before. It was our first and only homeless high tea. We loved doing things like this. It felt dangerous. Sometimes it *was* dangerous. For instance, I don't recommend going for a walk in your pyjamas late at night and accepting a lift to bikers' club houses to play pool. One of the things though about living on the edge is that occasionally you might fall off. As long as you can make the scramble back up, then you'll be okay.

Drake Street was not a five-bedroom house. It was a three-bedroom house with a study and a sunroom. In share-housing terms, that translates as a five bedder. Not five good bedrooms mind you, but five bedrooms nonetheless. My rent was a whopping $21 a week. That's because I had a window. Donna had a window, but her window led to Jo's room. Donna's room was probably meant to be the sewing room, or maybe it was once an airless nursery where a baby died of SIDS in the 1970s and the parents couldn't work out why. Jo's room wasn't actually a room: it was technically the entrance/sunroom. She pushed her bed up against the front door and the only entry to the house became the back door. Jo's room was a perfect display of hippy chic – fabric draped over the walls, hats, beads, and feathers hung from the ceiling – all placed in perfectly assembled chaos.

Di was the only person who had a proper bedroom with a double bed. The house was fully furnished and clearly one time belonged to a Greek family. (It wasn't just the completely concreted garden that gave this away, it was the landlord himself. He was Greek.) We made her pay $30 a week for the privilege of having not just a window that led outside, but a door. Although she had her own separate entrance in and out of her bedroom, she did have adjoining doors both to Rowena's room and Jo's room. I'd never seen so many connecting doors. Either the person who built it had trust issues, or they liked to hold wild swingers' parties.

While Jo had sealed the exit that led to her room with a dresser to deter unannounced mid-coital visits, the passage from Rowena's room was still open. Although the hefty $30 per week that Di paid meant that Rowena was supposed to use my room as access. Poor Rowena, her only access to and from her room was either through Di's room or mine. If we were both in compromising situations with spotty boys this meant Rowena had to either sleep on the couch or pick a door and run. Although Ro was pretty casual, she usually went for the door option, and it was not unusual for her to stop and peruse the chap in your bed. If she spotted a blackhead or two she'd have him pinned to the mattress in a power straddle, extracting blackheads. She loved squeezing blackheads. I guess some people might say it's Freudian, but knowing Rowena I'd just say it was less some repressed sexual behaviour and more of misunderstood talent. That girl could really clear a pore!

My room must have belonged to a kid. I had a cream-and-yellow laminex tiny single bed with built-in side tables and a two-door wardrobe with a full-length mirror in the middle. It was awful, and if I hadn't spent most of my time in that house drunk, stoned or on some sort of pill then I probably would have found it depressing. I did find out though, on one fateful occasion, that it was not a good room to take acid in. Or more accurately, to come down from acid. I remember lying on the bed when the side tables extended and the bed started to lift off the floor. Fire was coming out from under the sheets. Either I was burning up or there was a more logical explanation: my bed was a rocket. Laminex and acid are a powerful mix.

That particular night I remember having been cautious about slipping the half a tab of acid under my tongue. In no time at all I'd not only lost the power of speech, I was powerless to the effects of gravity. I could feel the tin walls of the nightclub I was in magnetising me. I literally couldn't pull myself off the wall for half the night. The only word I could manage to say was 'Gravity'. Acid is a strange author, the book it writes in your head is totally *Alice Through the Looking Glass*. If you've never taken acid and bent the fragile fractal of your mind's perception, then you won't have a clue what I am talking about. If you have, then you know how to smell colour. To take acid you need a robust mind. With a family history of anxiety and OCD I have one of those brains that could just simply decide to declare, 'I am an orange' and not come back. I remember reading about that happening to a university student somewhere in America and it terrified me. Although I guess not enough to stop me taking it.

We took a lot of drugs in that house. In fact, I am surprised I remember our time there at all. Drug-taking party houses are very different to the kind of house you have when you are a grown up. (Unless of course you are still taking drugs.) Drake Street was disgusting. I don't even know if that word does it justice. It was a health and safety risk. I am surprised *A Current Affair* never turned up to do a name and shame on us as 'the world's worst tenants'. Today I live in fear that if I ever become affluent enough to have a rental property I'll get my karmic retribution and get a bunch of house wreckers like us.

Today I can admit I am a cleaning obsessive. A chronic tidier. A compulsive wiper. But this wasn't always the case. There was a time when I wasn't only capable of creating extreme filth, I could also live in it. While I look back in horror at the thought of it, there's a part of me that wonders if I wasn't a lot more mentally well adjusted back then. Only a truly free spirit can live in chaos. Either that or you're well on the way to being either lazy or crazy or perhaps both.

It wasn't really our fault that Drake Street became a quagmire of filth. The house was ugly. And let's face it, it's hard to clean an ugly house. It's not like you'd clean the house and it's suddenly the Ritz. You clean a dump and it's still a dump, it's just a clean dump. Sometimes that just looks sadder. We certainly didn't care. Although once Donna sat on the steps and cried because she found the patch of carpet near the piano, 'poo corner', distressing. Poo corner was called poo corner because it was full of poo. Not human poo of course, cat poo. If you are going to enjoy the freedom of living out of home, eating cereal at night and drinking wine for breakfast than why not have a kitty kat too? Dianne already had a cat. I wanted one, so I got one, and so did Jo. At least Di's cat was toilet trained, or it was in the beginning and it was a boy. Jo and I got girl cats, and like us, they weren't desexed. Or house trained. The kitty litter was in the corner of the house just beyond the dining table. It was the only spot people didn't walk. The cats would have learnt to use the kitty litter if the girls owning the cats had been trained in cleaning the kitty litter. That tray would be full of pussy cat poo and none of us could face it. So we'd ignore it and wait for one of the other cat owners to buckle.

This meant that while we were all waiting, the cats would stop using the litter and start using the carpet around the litter. Eventually we'd just throw the tray out. Someone would be relegated the task of being gloved up on hands and knees scrubbing shit out of the polyester shag. But as you probably know shit sticks to shag, and good habits can be a long time coming in lazy girls. The cats just started shitting on the carpet. Then they had kittens. At one point we had 13 cats, all finding their way to poo corner. So I guess in a way we *had* toilet trained them. Poo corner was our personal watermark on how low we could all go when it came to shedding our good girl training. You see, we'd all found feminism, and this rejection of the patriarchal concept of clean was part of our liberation. Ironically, there was a house of three blokes just two doors down and their place was spotless. We thought they were wusses, and they once admitted they were frightened to visit us, but occasionally we'd wander down to their house, shag one of them and go home. We were like yobbo blokes. It was so much fun.

We rarely washed up. Dirty cups and plates littered every surface in the kitchen. If you wanted a cup of tea you needed a sterilising unit to make sure you didn't get Hepatitis B. Someone once suggested we 'should have a roster' and there was an outcry! How unfair and undemocratic it would be to create a purpose-built housework schedule when the current system of 'whose spirit breaks first cleans' seemed much more effective. Aforementioned pure of heart cleaning girl or girls would then get to lord it over the other lazy sluts for at least a week. We didn't have a neat little kitchen tidy bin, we had a proper sized outdoor bin in the kitchen and it was always spewing rubbish on the floor. Boxes filled with bottles. Dead goonsacks. And cigarette butts in everything. We smoked in the house, in bed, in every room, nearly every hour.

It was Queensland so in summer we battled maggots. On a bad day when you felt a tickle under your toes you'd take a peek and sure enough the whole floor would be a sea of larvae. This combined with the putrid stench of animal shit really made for some pungent summer odours. I guess we did our washing. But generally it was thrown on the floor in large piles. As were our towels. As was anything we didn't feel like dealing with. What started out as insane fun began to break us. After a year the cracks were showing.

Drake Street was our Ground Zero. I can't believe when we moved out we got some of our bond back. Honestly, the only way to rescue that place would have been to pressure hose it inside out. Coincidentally just a few months after we'd moved out the house burnt to the ground. The five of us were like the perfect storm. When we moved out into other share accommodation, none of us were ever able to replicate the same slum-like conditions we'd managed at Drake Street. There was some sort of dirty magic at work, and we were famous for it, party girls who'd become known in social circles as the Drake Street Girls. People I'd meet later would find out where I was living and they'd go, 'Oh, you are a Drake Street Girl.' I was never quite sure what they meant. Now I do. And fuck me, it was fun. Filthy, young, sexy beasts. Every girl should be a slovenly wench for at least one year of her life.

So this was my first proper living out of home experience. There were no aunts or cousins subletting me their spare room or garage. No mothers busting in every ten minutes crying and telling me to clean my room. This was where I got to cut my teeth on freedom. And looking back to being 17, I can't remember any greater feeling of freedom than turning the key (when I had it recut) and entering the house where I got to make the rules.

And the rule was, there were no rules.

Chaos in action.

Until I realised that some rules actually do help.

FENG SHITE

I don't have to believe in Feng Shui,
I do it because it makes me money.

Donald Trump

There are people who believe that your home and consequently your life is governed by forces you can't see. You may have paid thousands in therapy to try and push through some challenge in your life, but any numerologist will tell you there's nothing you can do. The problem is your house number. Like you don't want a karmic debt number. Anything that reduces to or adds up to 13, 14, 16 or 19 could see you on the way to financial ruin. But don't worry, apparently ruin is good for personal growth. Even the most fertile fields must lay fallow from time to time.

Understanding that your world is controlled by external forces beyond your control is the ultimate release for anyone who has ever wanted to opt out of taking responsibility for their life choices. It is such a relief to realise that poor financial management has more to do with your house number than your drug habit. So instead of addressing your issues, just address your address, and issue is resolved! Who said magic doesn't happen?

For those who prescribe to the Chinese practice of Feng Shui, a practice aimed at harmonising people with their environment, the key focus is not to make internal adjustments to change your life, just get your furniture placement right! If you do this then you could very well go on to live a long and happy life. I've always thought it a bit simplistic, although I have to admit there have been many times in my life when I wanted to blame my deeper problems on something as simple as where I put my bed. I mean, imagine if instead of 18 months of therapy all I needed was to move my nightstand and get rid of those candelabras with the pointy edges sending me 'Poison Arrows' in the night!

You aren't supposed to sleep with any pointy corners facing you. These are psychic arrows that will pierce your soul in the night. Everything facing the bed has to be soft and rounded. Kind of like a mental institution. So you can't hurt yourself. Or your imagined self.

There are so many rules when it comes to bed position and happiness that I can't seem to find anywhere remotely okay to put my bed.

Apparently sleeping with the bed directly opposite a mirror depletes your energy. I am not sure how the mirror does this. Maybe it has some sort of vampiric aspect that operates only at night. Maybe that's why vampires have no reflection. Because the mirror is the vampire. Wow, that's trippy, and there I was naively thinking the mirror was there to assist me match my trousers to my top so I didn't go out wearing a silk chemise and pearls with tracksuit pants.

According to Feng Shui experts, the mirror can also bring relationship troubles by introducing a 'third' person (generally known as your reflection, but trouble nonetheless). I've often suspected my husband of fooling around with my reflection. I mean, imagine the horror when I came home and found him butt naked making love to me! Talk about a betrayal!

The mirror can even make you depressed. I don't think there's been any actual clinical trials done linking mirrors facing beds to the incidence of depression, but I do agree that on waking and seeing myself first thing my immediate reaction is to shriek, 'Oh fuck!' It can take a bit to pick myself up after a shock like that – a person doesn't need to know what they look like on waking!

All my teenage girls sleep in rooms where their beds face the sliding mirror doors of their wardrobes! All this time I thought they slept a lot because they were lazy little shits, up all night on social media trawling for 'Likes' but as it turns out, it's because of the mirror sapping their energy. Apparently the solution is to hang a curtain over the mirrored doors at night so that they can wake up refreshed. Seems a bit Amish and frankly I couldn't be bothered. I didn't have the budget for another curtain outlay so I just asked the girls to sleep with their heads covered. The only drawback is they have to remember to take the head covering off before they enter any government buildings. Our conservative Government seems to consider head covering bad Feng Shui.

The other problem we have for Zoe's room is 'bed aligned with the door'. This also takes your energy away at night, supposedly because the door resembles the shape of a coffin, which is always carried feet first. They sure say some creepy shit. Great. All five kids desperately wanted their own room and to be able to do this we had to go a little smaller on the room size, so when it comes to applying Feng Shui there's just not that much room for negotiation. You put the bed where it fits and you lie down. End of story.

One of Zoe's walls is a sliding mirror door wardrobe. The other walls are two long windows facing the mountain. The fourth wall faces the windows looking at the mountain. She sleeps against a window, and faces the mirror and the doorway. What am I doing to this poor kid! I am surprised she wakes up at all. I can't work out how to remedy this, so instead in the meantime I've asked her to sleep on the couch.

And for all of you who have installed ceiling fans. Go rip them out. They're bad Feng Shui too. The only thing that should be hung above the bed is a soft canopy. I guess this is based on the theory that anything heavy hanging above you is liable to fall on you and kill you. This is a bit silly. I think you have to consider that our health and safety standards have improved since Feng Shui was invented 4000 years ago. In the old days sleeping under a rusted iron candelabra held in place with some sheep intestine probably did put the sleeper at considerable risk, but these days things have been installed by licensed operators. We don't use sheep gut or wool to fix things to the ceiling anymore. Unless they are on special at Bunnings.

Personally though, I don't like things hanging over my head when I sleep. There have been times in the past sleeping in a low-ceiling motel room with the fan on a lopsided rotation that I imagined a spectacular death where the fan came away from the ceiling and disembowelled me in my sleep. Then I woke up with some bloke whose name I couldn't remember and thought, 'Christ I wish that fan would come away from the ceiling and kill me now'.

I didn't install fans in our new house because I thought they look ugly. Is that shallow? It's not just the cumbersome helicopter on the ceiling feeling they create, it's that they always fill up with dust and weird sticky grime. It fills me with anxiety. I once said to my husband during sex, 'If you don't get your sock onto that fan and clean the blade I'll never climax.'

Being able to view undusted areas from my bed is very distracting for me. So I decided we could all suffer our stifling summers fan free. I mean, people pay to go to saunas, how would this be any different! Imagine the bonus detoxification of sweating it out EVERY night! My husband agreed but suggested that it was a little unreasonable considering we live in the tropics. I can't tell you how delighted I was to let him know a few months down the track that while I might have fucked up all the other Feng Shui alignments, I got that one right. I mean, wouldn't you rather be hot than deal with 'bad' energy?

I am not quite sure what bad energy is. People who do Feng Shui talk a lot about bad energy. I think bad energy basically means poor, ugly, fat, angry, sick, lonely and unhappy. Wow, aren't those the seven dwarfs we all know and love! Sounds like a pretty normal family group to me. If we can move our bed ten centimetres to the left to avoid any of those consequences then most of us are happy to oblige.

The literature around Feng Shui also implies bad energy can cause poor communication and relationship issues. Imagine struggling to love your partner only to find out it wasn't you, or even him, it was the fucking fan! And it's not just the fan getting the blame for relationship woes, apparently hanging from the chandeliers is out, especially if it's hanging above your bed. So I kind of stuffed that one up. While I didn't install fans I got each of the kids to choose a funky pendant/chandelier style light fitting that hangs from the ceiling in the middle of their rooms – pretty well smack bang over their beds. Looks like they've got poor health and broken relationships to look forward to. 'Thanks Mum!'

Oh and I should mention you can't sleep under the window. You need a wall behind your bed because otherwise your energy is going to get weaker and weaker and weaker. That's right, the window is going to make you fade like old curtains in the sun. Your energy is going to seep out of your head and by morning you may not even be there. Just a stain on the mattress where you once were. An outline. Like the chalk outline on a cop show when there's been a body that's been taken away. That's what the window will do to you.

Sloping ceilings are also a bit of a no no. Apparently the sloped ceiling will hinder the nighttime rejuvenation process that happens when you sleep. You may end up suffering from emotional instability and low energy. This is bad news for anyone living in an A-frame house, a tepee or a caravan. From the time I spent in a caravan park on family holidays I can attest that there certainly seemed to be a lot more emotionally unstable people per square metre than one would have considered usual – but stupid me had put that down to excessive alcohol consumption. It was not that at all. It was the slopey roof of the bloody van.

Now while you are struggling to organise your bedroom so you don't completely fuck your life, you also must realise bed access can be an issue. If you can only access your bed from one side, then you are limiting the energy flow of your bed. Partners may feel trapped – like they are metaphorically and literally up against the wall. In order to have a harmonious relationship, your partner needs to be able to leave of their own free will. So try not to wedge them against the wall. Unless you're the needy type and that's the only way you can stop them doing a runner.

You also can't sleep too close to the door. Another energy flow problem. I was having so many problems with the Feng Shui on Zoe's room, particularly around the whole door issue, I ripped it off and got the plasterer around to seal up the door-shaped hole. So now it's not a door – it's a wall. The Feng Shui has improved slightly but she's stuck inside. I think that's okay. For every problem there is a Feng Shui solution. So now I just feed her through the window. And toileting is not a problem, we just need a nice bucket. With a lid, of course. And I will have to get the colour right. And it should be metal. Hmm, or should I be going for wood?

I don't know, maybe I'm just a jaded old cynic, but I get the feeling that if I want to change my life, I have to do more than move my bed. I have to change the idiot who lies in it. Me. Feng Shui that, master!

THE LONG WAY HOME

We just can't stop people from being homeless
if that's their choice ...

Tony Abbott, Australian Prime Minister

You can't write a book about place, or more specifically 'home', without reflecting on what it means to be without a home. I must at this point acknowledge that this book has been written from the middle-class comfort of my home office on one of the seven computers that belong to our family. I had never really counted them before, and while one of them is supplied by my daughter's school, and another has been supplied by the newspaper I work for one day a week, it strikes me that we are a lot more materially abundant than most, yet possibly a lot less than some. Wealth and financial security tends to be 'aspirational', so one tends to measure one's own worth looking 'up' rather than 'down'.

In comparison to how most Australians – and most of the world – lives, I am rich. Sure we probably spend more than we earn, we don't have investment properties, stock portfolios, holiday houses or fabulous overseas holidays, but we have two cars, a six-bedroom mortgage and enough earnings to feed the monster. I call debt 'the monster'. In my experience, the more I earn and the more children I have, the bigger the monster gets, and the harder I have to work to feed it. Just when I think the monster is fed for the week it starts growling again via unpaid road tolls, water rates, school fees, dental bills, dry cleaning, car servicing, insurance payments, phone bills. It's the constant stream of consumption that keeps the system running.

Comparatively, I don't consider us to be an affluent family. After all, we still haven't managed to scrape the funds together to build the in-ground pool. To me, having a pool is the affluence marker. When I was a kid if you had a pool you'd made it. And I don't mean an inflatable. I mean a proper pool. End of story. Somehow I still have that stored subconsciously. It used to be families aspired to having a television or an inside toilet. For me, it's a pool. People come over and say, 'I love your house, you've done a great job with the build. It's beautiful.' And I say, 'Thanks, we're really happy. Although we don't have a pool. Yet.' Of course the plans are afoot, and ironically the act of attaining the signifier of wealth, aka the pool, will in fact cause us to sustain increased and ongoing debt. Such is the nature of the monster that is capitalism.

I am guilty of forgetting to be grateful. As I kneel at the altar of endless want, I do tend to focus more on what I don't have than what I do. I have to remember to remind myself to be thankful for my soft fluffy towels, my crisp white linen, my Country Road quilt covers, my cushions, my 12-seater leather lounge, my pillow-top king-size mattress, my big screen telly.

My six bedrooms full of lovely useless things for my lovely useless children. If I ever sleep outdoors it's not because I've fallen on hard times, it's because I've fallen asleep on a daybed.

While I may have grown up on struggle street, and indeed have visited it a number of times as an adult woman, these days I live on the 'other' side of town. I no longer stand at the supermarket internally adding up the cost of my groceries to make sure I stay under my $100 weekly shopping budget so as to avoid the embarrassment of putting things back. If you've ever had to do that, it's humiliating.

At least I suppose the only witness is a 16-year-old on minimum wage. I have had to put back shampoo, conditioner, sanitary products. All the non-essentials. After all, unwashed hair will eventually stabilise and create its own ecosystem and when it comes to sanitary products, I guess there's always the reusing of old towels. You can even reframe your economic hardship by saying, 'I have decided to engage in sustainable environmentally friendly practices. Used tampons are choking our oceans.' When you're walking around the house with a scratchy old bit of towel shoved down your undies, environmental smugness can help relieve the discomfort.

My new middle class circumstance has meant that I have redefined what it means to struggle. We still do it tight. But we do it tight with very nice food and wine, trips to the hairdresser and a latte every morning at the coffee shop. The weekly shopping bill for my family of seven generally totals $500. For some families, this is their entire weekly income. While I always attempt some sort of expenditure restraint with my '100 ways with mince' meal planning, I think nothing of throwing a $12 tub of Persian fetta in my trolley. And while I'm at it, a slab of blue castello. And some olives. And a tub of sundried tomatoes. This is middle-class food. The deli was a no-go zone when I was a single mum. If I went there I wouldn't be able to afford cigarettes.

I hate the way people judge poor people. Like because you're shit broke you're not allowed to make bad decisions. Bad decisions are reserved for rich pricks who can afford it. I only smoked when I couldn't afford it. I still don't entirely understand the psychology of smoking. I do know that poor people get shit all the time for spending welfare on booze and cigarettes. And while I agree that, yes, it's definitely bad money management and creates greater health disadvantages for you and your kids, I understand that spending welfare on booze and cigarettes does help you forget you are on welfare. In fact, I think even with the tax increases, booze and cigarettes are still cheaper than health food. Healthy organic food is only for the affluent. The poor get hot chips. And sauce. That's two food groups at least. Add a ciggie and you've got three.

I have read *The Life You Can Save*, Peter Singer's savagely stinging economic treatise on first world over indulgence and the questionable morals of people like me who don't give their money away. Or at least enough of it to make a difference. According to Singer, for us to be economically ethical we should be giving away more than half our income to charity. The problem is, I agree. In theory. Like most people who have learnt to live beyond their means, I can't imagine how I am supposed to do it. 'Mr Singer, do you mean I should cancel the cleaners who come here once a week, get rid of one of the cars, downsize to a caravan and use scratchy towels?' I don't want to seem like a cruel-hearted capitalist, but I can't do it. I can't seem to cut back. Does that mean I have to let myself go grey? No waxing? Or spray tans? I don't know if the world needs more grey-haired, hairy white women. I am all for sharing the wealth for the greater good, but must I let myself go? I do make a small deposit in the morality bank by cooking dessert for a soup kitchen every month – does that count?

It's hard to enjoy the fruits of your labour, or should I say 'privilege' when you know it's built on the back of someone else's suffering. That's how the capitalist system works. Perpetual growth, wealth creation and of course lots and lots of poverty. There can't be enough wealth for everyone because otherwise the whole aspirational, work harder, strive, strive, strive system would fall on its arse.

So how can I truly enjoy my fortunate circumstance, knowing that there are many out there who don't have a roof over their head? I can tell myself it's because I worked hard, and I deserved it. That ideology irks me because, without saying it explicitly, we demonise the 'poor' by insinuating that they also get what they deserve, because they must have failed to work hard or be drug addicts or filthy scum. I just can't reconcile the values of my good Catholic upbringing with this mindset. I can't make this okay. Every human being, regardless of circumstance deserves a safe place to live. Everyone needs a home.

In Maslow's triangle of need, home is on the second rung as an essential requirement for us to be healthy happy humans. Home isn't just about real estate. It's about personal security – a place where a person can retreat – the cornerstone for a person's identity and sense of self. So what happens when you don't have this? How does a person maintain a sense of who they are and why they are important when they are sleeping on a park bench? Perhaps this is why we don't 'see' homelessness, because in their own eyes, and in ours, they don't exist. It occurred to me in writing this book that our sense of home and our sense of going home is intrinsically connected with our deeper sense of who we are. Returning home is what we do each day to recuperate and regroup before we face the world again. In the return to the physical bricks and mortar of our actual homes, we also engage in a more spiritual process of a 'return to self'. It's no surprise that mental health problems, social isolation and alienation are some of the issues facing the homeless.

I have only ever really been homeless for one night. It was when I was at university and it was during that crossover period between one residence and the next. My best friend Jo and I had to sleep in someone's driveway. In a car, I might add. We didn't just lie down on the concrete. We may have been students but we at least had reclining seats. It was uncomfortable, but I imagined it was good training for a long haul flight if I ever made it overseas. We even wore circulation socks to prevent DVT.

We woke up with the faces of the Vietnamese family who lived there, pressed up against the glass window of the car staring in at us, wondering why two strangely dressed white girls had passed out in their driveway. I realise now that it must have been a bit shocking for them to find us there – for a second, they must have thought we were both dead. God knows we certainly looked it. We'd decided the best way to ensure a full night's sleep was to get really drunk. We'd drained an entire 2-litre cask of wine. In the morning I remember having to wipe the dribble from the corner of my mouth before I levered the seat up to sitting position. The smallest child looking in screamed when the dead white girl suddenly popped up into view. It took a while to rouse Jo, who was in the driver's seat, but once she became at least semi-conscious we drove to our new premise and parked there until the landlord arrived with the key. I don't know why we didn't park in that driveway in the first place. Or go to a backpackers.

I have met people who have lived in their cars for weeks and, in some cases, months. For many Australians this is the only 'housing' option they are left with. My one night as a student gave me a tiny taste of what this must be like. It was uncomfortable, unpredicatable and, I imagine in some occasions, actually unsafe.

In comparison to sleeping rough however, a car would be a better option. I have slept rough twice. Once was when I attended Maleny Festival to perform in a two-hander with my fellow performer Stella. We were booked for two nights and it didn't occur to us that we were supposed to bring a tent. We slept on a towel on the grass. The mosquitoes were a bit of a problem, then the hardness of the ground started to make my body ache. Every time I turned over I found a new rock. Once again we retreated to the bar to get drunk enough to pass out deeply enough to ignore the discomfort. I certainly understand why some homeless people drink. Whether or not it got them to that end destination, alcohol seems like a sensible solution when you're sleeping on the ground. That early morning dew is a killer. Sleeping under the stars may seem romantic, but you tend to wake up wet. I guess that's why cowboys slept around fires and not empty goon sacks.

The other time I slept rough happened in Sydney. Not as hippified or benevolent as a folk festival. I'd been staying with a new boyfriend in Glebe. As it turned out, when I went to dinner with friends at a nearby restaurant he took the opportunity to go visit his previous and possibly still very current girlfriend who lived in Chatswood. Somehow I managed a drunken stumble through a park and some back streets to find his house. It was one of those semi-detached terrace houses. Windows were barred. Doors were tripple locked. It was 1 am, his flatmates were asleep and he was AWOL. I knocked on the door. No answer. I knocked on the door again. Still no answer. I pounded. I yelled. I threw rocks at the window. Then I tried to climb onto the second floor balcony by climbing up the downpipe. It was my first foray into pole dancing and a brutal reminder that 90 kilo women are earthbound. I made it about 3 feet off the ground before the metal that held the pipe to the brickwork gave way and the pipe came away from the wall.

I'd ripped my dress. I'd cut my leg. I tore the hem off my dress and tied it around my shin to stop the bleeding. I was still drunk. It seems alcohol and my incidents of temporary homelessness have some sort of correlation. I started crying in panic. This was the time before mobile phones. This was my first time in Sydney. I was certain that I would be raped and possibly murdered. Then a glimmer of hope. My boyfriend's window was open and on the ground floor. And I could see a phone. Sure there were bars on the window but if I stretched far enough I could just reach it. Then I realised – I didn't know anyone's phone number in Sydney to call for help. I didn't think my boyfriend's flatmates would appreciate a triple 0 call resulting in the police axeing the door down just to let me in.

Injured, thirsty and alone, I drank straight out of the hose, pulled the bin up close to the front of the house usually reserved for rubbish or bikes, found some cardboard and made myself a bed, using the bin as a baricade. All I had for comfort was one bent cigarette and a couple of matches. On lighting the cigarette I was reminded of one of my favourite children's stories, *The Little Match Girl*. Here I was at 18 curled up near a bin living out the poignant grown-up version, possibly renamed *The Little Drunk Girl*. When my boyfriend returned early that morning from his romantic nocturnal ramblings, he discovered a homeless girl curled up in cardboard behind the bin. He joked about me being 'white trash' and helped me up. I wasn't in a good mood. He kissed me on the forehead and I returned his warmth with a 'Go fuck yourself.' That night I discovered why some homeless people mutter agitatedly to themselves or appear angry for no reason. They have plenty of reasons. For people without keys to anywhere remotely safe, the night is a scary place.

While I haven't ever experienced long-term homelessness, I have lived in some pretty substandard accommodation. Like when I left a two-year relationship with one of the most sociopathic men I've ever met in my life. The dude had me ironing his sheets and writing his university assignments while he watched *The Simpsons*. One day he actually complained because the assignment I wrote for him only got a credit instead of a distinction. I think that was the moment I realised that the relationship scored an uncontestable FAIL and I packed what was left of my belongings into a suitcase and wheeled it down the road. I had $15 in my wallet and nothing in the bank because he had taken everything. I knocked on the front door of a house that I'd seen 'alternative' type singles coming and going from and asked, 'Can I live in your shed? I can pay $15.' I was then led to this creepy little spider-infested snake pit in the backyard. One of the singles kindly donated a single foam mattress and that became home. I am convinced it was a hovel made entirely of broken asbestos. When you don't have a choice you don't tend to worry so much about longterm health risks.

Everywhere from that has pretty well been up. Looking back, I realise my brain could have snapped at that moment. I was so close to the edge. Abusive relationship, new in town, no friends, no money and an absolutely demolished self-esteem. I was on my horse and heading straight for crazy town. I stood on the precipice of the abyss, smoked a joint, and narrowly avoided falling in. Six weeks later I'd saved enough money for rent and bond for a proper room in a share house by the beach. Finally, I was a real person again.

There is nothing more soul destroying than being rejected by the people in a share house. If it's a job or a bank loan, then I can understand it – those are real measurable criteria that I am failing to meet. But failing one of those awful share house interviews is really bad for a person's self-esteem. You fail essentially because people don't like you. They decide you would be no good to live with. It's a little surreal sitting around a coffee table drinking herbal tea while people tell you, 'We don't smoke, don't drink, don't take drugs, don't eat meat or dairy but apart from that we really encourage people to be themselves.' I could tell from the moment I asked, 'Do you have an ashtray?' that I was deemed 'not spiritual enough'.

Once I worked out that every 'meet and greet' with a prospective house buddy was in fact an audition, I started to mirror back what people want to hear. It's a very successful technique. People are attracted to people who are like them. Instead of answering questions, I started asking about them. Pretending I was actually interested in their banal lives. It worked. I got to live with whatever dickheads I wanted to. Some of them are still my very, very good friends. Well, at least until this paragraph when I called them dickheads.

As my children now wander out into the housing market seeking shelter, I wonder how they are going to fare. For many young people, the prospect of ever owning their own home is remote. I didn't own my own home until I was 43. I thought I'd missed the housing boat as well. It's funny how people kind of assume that if you look middle aged, middle class and middle of the road, that you must be a home owner. It's like assuming a couple with children is married or that all the children are biologically theirs, or that they're even a couple. It's a convention – like a tick in the box on the checklist for 'normal' for John and Jane Citizen.

I can't tell you how many people have visited me in my rental properties over the years and asked me if I'd considered selling. I always replied, 'Yes, I've considered it. But it would probably piss the owners off.' They'd laugh uncomfortably and I'd laugh uncomfortably because I felt like I had been through an instant financial audit and received a little tick on the 'financial loser' box. When you're 20 not owning your own home is not an issue. At 30 there's a question mark, and by 40 you might have some explaining to do.

People are suspicious of the 'poor'. Which is ironic really, because as shown by the recent ICAC investigations when it comes to integrity, we have a lot more to worry about with affluent people.

I don't know how anyone who's young, or who's had a bad run, or is down on their luck could get a rental lease right now. In the old days when you wanted to rent a property, providing you hadn't torched your previous address, you were told the address and given the key. These days you have to participate in the real estate agent's 'Prove you're not a loser' test. It's like a financial, psychological and employment pap smear.

Recently an old friend of mine used me as a character reference for a property she and her partner had applied to rent. They are both in their late 40s with jobs. She and her partner had been requested to provide a total of four personal references each. That's eight people in total. Of course employer details were required, as was the last 20 to 30 years of her housing history, her and her partner's bank account details, plus photocopies of bank statements showing the balance. I'm surprised they didn't ask for a mental health check, blood samples and an anal probe. Not long afterwards I get the phone call from Rebecca. (Rebecca would be pushing 18, tops.)

Poor Rebecca has the dubious task of ringing the eight character references and performing a rather embarrassing cross examination. The first question was acceptable. 'How long have you known the applicant?'

'Um, 30 years.' Before Rebecca was born. Probably before her own father had pubic hair.

Rebecca's next question was more personal. 'Have you ever been to a house where the applicant has lived and if so can you tell me how she kept the house.' Wow. I could be a serial hoarder for all Rebecca knows, living in a pile of newspapers surrounded by cats. I mean, who am I to judge?

'Yes I have. She is very tidy, always does the dishes, makes her beds and keeps the house very clean. She's a grown woman. I think she's been cleaning a home for over three decades so she's got pretty good at it.'

I can hear Rebecca breathing. I don't think she knows which box to check. So I kept going. 'There was this one time though when she left the milk on the bench. Overnight.' Rebecca doesn't say anything. The evil part of me wants to add, 'Oh and every once and a while she likes to smear poo on the walls, but apart from that, she's super tidy!'

Then Rebecca asks something unexpected. 'What kind of person is she? How would you describe her?'

Really? This is beginning to feel like I am helping to compile an online dating profile, not provide a rental reference. I am not sure what to say.

'She's very kind. Intelligent. Funny. And a nympho. She will turn the garage into a sex dungeon, but don't worry, she hoses it out once a week.' Then I realise what Rebecca was fishing for. 'She's reliable, hardworking, honest and has a lot of integrity.' It was getting more patronising by the moment. 'She's been in upper management positions for 20 years, Rebecca.'

'Oh, that sounds good.' Rebecca is typing, I hear the clatter of the keyboard. I get to thinking the only upper management position poor Rebecca has experienced so far is missionary. How cruel of estate agents to get the newest recruits to do the dirtiest work.

Rebecca hasn't finished. There's one more line of enquiry.

'Do you know her cat?'

Well I've patted it once or twice, but do I know it? Does anyone ever really KNOW a cat? If James Packer applied to lease a property would Rebecca be calling up his best mate David Gyngell to ask what kind of bloke he was and had he met his cat? 'Well Rebecca, he's prone to punch ups and he likes a lot of pussy.' I doubt it. 'Yes, I have met her cat.'

Then Rebecca goes one step further into a line of questioning that even I didn't expect. 'And how would you describe its toileting?'

'Excuse me?'

Rebecca qualifies her question: 'How is she with the kitty litter?'

You know, when I visit someone, that's the first place I go to look. The kitty litter.

The paranoid part of my brain starts to panic – has Rebecca heard about poo corner?

'She's excellent Rebecca, my friend hardly ever misses.' There is silence. 'Oh, you mean the cat?' There is beeping. Rebecca has hung up.

How am I going to tell my friend that my kitty litter joke may have made her homeless? How much information does someone need to take your money?

Having your own home was once the great Australian dream. It seems it's evolved into great Australian fantasy. Soon to be the sad Australian myth.

Everyone deserves a place to live. May I suggest a solution in response to Tony Abbott's compassion challenged statement: *'We just can't stop people from being homeless if that's their choice.'* Perhaps those same people who 'choose' to be homeless might consider taking up residence at one of the many spare rooms at The Lodge in Canberra or for Sydney's homeless, there's always Kirribilli House.

I mean, you can't stop people moving into public property if that's their choice.

THE PEOPLE IN YOUR STREET

Watching television is like taking black spray paint to your third eye.

Bill Hicks

Ever since I was a kid one of my favourite pastimes was looking in people's houses. I don't mean being actually invited in to have a look. I mean having a sneaky glance through a window or an open door. There's nothing more exciting than seeing something that you were not supposed to see. Like life's freeze frame. I guess it could be seen as voyeuristic – some might even call it a bit stalky. I don't think so though. It's just a bit inappropriate, that's all. I have never looked for a long time. And I certainly don't take photographs. It has never occurred to me to commit what I see to film. The mental snapshot is always enough.

It's this freaky little game I play. I call it, 'Imagine being them.' I do it when I'm walking past people's houses on a casual afternoon or morning stroll. And as I walk past I have a sticky-beak inside people's houses, what I can see of them going about their lives, either eating lunch, or reading, or cooking, or more often than not just sitting in silence watching television. I see them in their place, the nest they've made away from the hustle of the everyday and you get this picture of the private person. Then I imagine I'm them. That I'm the old man sitting on that Jason recliner watching the news eating my steak, and that the woman in the kitchen whose slipper I can only just see is my wife and she's going to be bringing me a beer, or maybe a cup of tea. For an instant I live in the house in their life. I generally get some sort of emotional response, and more often than not I'll shake it off with an, 'Oh, I'm glad I'm not them,' and then I move onto the next house.

I should add that I don't stop and stare. This exercise isn't done with that much focus – these are just the thoughts that drift in and out of my very dramatic, and often very judgemental inner monologue. I do realise that I know nothing about these people and that it's entirely unfair to be jumping to conclusions about the amazingness or the futility of their lives all based on one glance, but it doesn't *really* matter because it's just something I do to keep myself amused. I don't actually know any of these people. That would wreck the game, because then I'd have too much information and I wouldn't be able to engage in my fiction-creating perambulation.

I don't know why I do this. I guess it's a bit weird. I've never really thought about it until now. There wasn't much on telly when I was a kid and we often used to go for an evening gloat. My mother liked looking in at people's lives too. The best time to watch people without them knowing is at night. The dark gives people an illusion of discretion and anonymity, but in reality the only person who's anonymous is the pervert standing in the bushes watching you brush your teeth imaging that those teeth were hers. That she would then walk into the other room and join her family and resume her life. I'm not a creep. For the record I've never watched anyone have sex. I've just watched people living, talking, sitting, reading, dancing, singing, crying. It's a spectacularly fascinating activity. Who needs to have some sort of 'living installation' simulated at a modern art gallery or in the guise of reality TV when people are living lives everywhere all over this planet and all you have to do is look?

My favourite place to do the late night pervy walk is caravan parks. Oh they just bring out the Diane Arbus in me. Every little van seems to have some sort of Arbus-esque type scenario. Fat women in bras washing their undies in the sink, gnarly old grey-haired men cutting their toenails on the caravan step, a young bloke covered in tatts with an orange mullet cutting up fish, three old friends playing cards, women screaming at their teenage daughters, children sleeping lit only by the TV glow of *CSI* or some other loud violent crime show, a morbidly obese family fighting over who gets the chicken leg. I love it. I pretend to be all of them. Usually it ends with the mantra 'Glad I'm not them.' I know it seems unkind, but it's quite a neat way of appreciating your own humble life. There are times though when you play the game and you end up feeling a bit depressed because their imagined lives are so lovely you don't want to come home. The trick of the game is to make sure every scenario has a poignant twist. I make that up so I get to feel better than the person I'm watching. I think in bible terms it's known as 'coveting thy neighbour's arse'. In real terms it's just a bit of harmless gloating, because I'm actually doing the opposite of coveting.

I often think about humans living together in such close physical proximity but not actually knowing anything about each other. It seems bizarre that you can live on top of each other for years and have barely said hello. Hear someone's footsteps thudding gently on the floor above and never see their face. It seems kind of unnatural to me. I guess that's because I'm a country girl.

An old boyfriend of mine used to love saying about high-density housing, 'Why do they call them apartments when they are so close together?' It's a good point. Although I think the 'apart' sentiment was less about the physical separation of the housing and more about the physical separation of the people. These are places where people get lonely. So many people so close together all with so little meaningful contact.

When I was living in semi-detached housing in one of Sydney's inner suburbs, I used to imagine what would happen if suddenly we took the walls away. Or if the walls that delineated one house from another were made of glass. We were living like human rats in our little human rat boxes, sleeping with our heads pressed up against opposite sides of the same wall but never actually getting to know who the other rat was. The entire time I lived in that street I never got to see my neighbours. It's like they'd poke their little rat heads out of their doors to check if the coast was clear and make a bolt for the car.

I knew they had children. I heard them being rounded up into the car early in the mornings and unloaded in the evenings. I never saw any of them. But I could hear them. I used to hear the husband yell at her. And then she'd cry. I wanted to tap on the wall, maybe go to the door and ask if she was ok, but there's this social code when you live in urban settings that you pretend the other people aren't there. I played the same game I played with my slice of life snapshots, but this time I had to construct stories and pictures of the life from what I heard. Somehow what I heard ended up being a lot more heartbreaking than the bits and pieces in my perve bank.

I found this whole city approach of pretending other people weren't there a bit perplexing. I never managed to do it very well, I kept forgetting that you aren't really supposed to interact with people on trains or buses, or on the street or in shops standing near you at the counter. I think I often came across as needy or crazy. Which meant instead of disarming people with my friendliness, my smile, or my heartfelt remark about the jolliness of their new baby, I was often met with a look of terror and visible thoughts of, 'Is this woman a threat?' 'What does she want?' 'Why is she talking to us and commenting on our baby?' 'Don't smile back.' I'd be compelled to withdraw and left feeling a bit embarrassed – like when you say hello to someone who you thought you knew and then realise half way through an overly exuberant and extremely familiar greeting that you have never met them and are left explaining to the person who clearly couldn't give a shit how much they look like this old friend of yours. Clearly if you can't recognise the old friend, then they mustn't have really been much of a friend so you just end up looking like a loser on all counts.

I tried to pretend people weren't there. But I am what I call an interventionist. I am always getting involved. If someone drops something I'll stop and help them pick it up. If a pram needs lifting up a staircase, I'm right there. I attempt to help cranky old ladies on walking frames cross the road even when they snap 'I can do this myself. I'm very independent.' And I snap back, 'Listen bitch, this is about me, not you!'

After a few years of living in Sydney I found that, like the other zombies, I was starting to disappear into the pretend personal space. Sitting on a bus completely oblivious to a woman having a little sob next to me. I understand why people do this, but I just think it's stupid. If you don't like people, then don't live with so many of them. Live in the desert. I think if you are going to live surrounded by people you should make an effort to take notice of them. Maybe don't walk past their homes at night tyring to catch them in their undies so you can pretend you are them, but maybe try some sort of other empathy or compassion activation exercise. Like saying something really challenging like: 'Are you okay?'

When I moved into my current neighbourhood a woman who lives down the road came around with homemade brownies. It was a simple and delightful display of welcome. Sadly, in many of our cities, if someone did this you'd be throwing the brownies in the bin declaring 'some crazy bitch dropped these off – they're probably full of rat poison! Or worse, gluten!' It's a bit sad when you start living with a belief that you must protect yourself from the worst in people. That you'd have to fear there was something sinister about the brownies, rather than something good.

One of the things I love about where we live is the neighbourhood. We live in a new suburb, in fact we were like the second or third house on the block. In a year 11 houses sprang up. Now two years later there's around 30; over the next few years there'll be a few hundred more. Being part of the first 11 gave us a 'fences down' approach. This meant children found their way to each other without need of the local park or something as formal as play dates. They simply went outside and said, 'Do you want to go and climb that tree?' And they were off. In fact there's even a tree that the kids in the neighbourhood have claimed as their own. It's ironic sometimes to see the impressive park empty and the modest tree with a hand made swing and fort and prayer flags full of kids.

Unlike the city where people lived anonymously behind walls, here we were in full visibility of everyone in the hood. In fact, at night when we sit around the table for dinner I have been told that people a few streets away can see us. I kind of like that. Now I'm a person in a house that someone else can watch as I clear the table, sweep the floor and yell at the kids and they'll think, 'Imagine being her.'

I guess, in a way I'm lucky, because I am. 'Her', that is. It's in those moments, engaged in the daily grind, doing normal everyday things with my normal everyday kids, in my normal everyday house, I catch sight of my own reflection in the night glass of the windows and I remind myself of how very very lucky I am.

Covet that you silly bitch.

HOME ALONE

My maternal grandmother, Thelma, lived alone. Once her children left and her husband died, she lived forty years by herself, a small tidy woman in a big old Queenslander. It seemed to suit her. She was shy and socially withdrawn, an unusual mix of German stoicism, mixed with superstition and sweetness. She was well used to her own company. I often wondered if she was lonely, as she moved wordlessly about her large empty house. I wondered if she had just accepted loneliness as her lot. She never seemed to have friends. She was far too shy for that. And other people generally annoyed her. Although she was a very quiet woman, she had a surprisingly wicked sense of humour. I wondered how a woman who loved to laugh could spend so much time on her own. She did have a few social outings. She caught the bus into town once a week to do her shopping. On Sundays she visited her brother Fred, who lived alone in the house she'd grown up in. She'd roast him a chicken and watch the clock until it was time for home. Her younger brother Douglas would drop off a copy of the *Chronicle*, the local daily rag, in the late afternoon. And apart from visits from her children and their grandchildren, which was generally only a few times a year, that was basically it. For the rest of the week she didn't go out. She didn't play bingo, or bowls, or go to church. She stayed home.

Thelma loved summer. She'd take up residence in the lounge room and watch the entire Ashes test. It seemed like the leisure choice of a fat old man drinking beer, not a petite grandmother sipping her tea. TV was company for Thelma. She certainly had her favourite programs. Like *Prisoner*. Maybe it wasn't so unusual that she related to the soap opera of women living 'on the inside'. Thelma had been doing solitary for years.

She used to talk to the television. As a child this made staying at her house rather amusing. We'd be watching a drama and a character would go to meet someone in a park and she'd shout, 'Don't sit there! Can't you see there's a man behind that tree with a gun!' She called women who loved bad men 'stupid' and the bad men 'bastards'. She lived by routine. Up at 6 am. Breakfast of tea and toast. Morning tea at 10.30 am. Lunch at 12. On the dot, mind you. Afternoon tea of tea and biscuit at 3 pm. Dinner at 5.30 pm. Dinner was early because 6 pm = the ABC news. Thelma had always eaten, cleared the table and washed up by news time.

She was fastidious about meals being on time. In fact, she became anxious if they were even ten minutes off schedule. It's not like anyone was hassling her with, 'I'm hungry … when's dinner?' When I think of my grandmother's tight meal delivery regime I feel like a lazy old slut. Every time my kids ask when's dinner, and I reckon there would be a series of questions like that asked in five-minute increments, I say, 'In about 20 minutes.' I keep saying this until around 8 pm, the time when I actually get dinner on the table.

If the evening meal had hit the table at 8 pm Thelma would have dropped dead from anxiety. She had no pets, just a few orchids, and every day she pushed her way through the identical routine. I would have gone fucking nuts. For a tiny woman, I think Thel was a lot tougher than she looked.

Don't get me wrong, I tend to live by routine too, but I have children, a husband and my own work life to manage. The routine is a structure I try and adhere to so the kids have clean undies, lunches and bus money. Thelma didn't have anyone to manage except herself. Why, if she wanted to, she could sleep until noon. But that would never, ever, ever, ever happen. Thelma was an early riser. Every night she would go to bed at 10 pm, regardless of whether or not she was watching a gripping program on TV. She would not stay up five minutes longer, because bed was at 10. Not half past or ten past or five past.

I don't think I'd handle living alone as well as Thelma. I think it takes guts. And mental tenacity. A person's mind can wander to some pretty freaky places when they're on their own. Whenever I've lived on my own I can't stop thinking someone is coming to rape and murder me. Of course I only worry about this at night.

It doesn't occur to me that it's probably just as likely for a person to be raped and murdered in the day, but it's only when the lights are off and you are lying there hearing every frickin' sound do you think, 'What was that? That was someone sharpening a knife,' or 'That was someone pushing open a window,' and the next minute the cat jumps on the bed and you shit yourself.

When I lived alone I pulled the curtains and locked the doors every night. Heck, I even put a chair up against my door to stop all the super keen rapists from getting me. I had always thought I was a very confident, self-assured person. But the first night on my own pretty well told me a very different story. I am neurotic, insecure and unstable. Clearly, I do better living with other people. Personally I prefer living with confident self-assured people as large groups of unstable neurotics are just too much hard work.

Living alone makes it much harder to find someone to blame. My couple of stints solo taught me how hard it is to clean up when no-one else is there. What is the point of being a martyr if there aren't any witnesses? Suffering is pointless if no-one sees it.

I can certainly see how easy it would be to become a crazy cat lady living in a nest made of old newspapers. When I lived alone I tended to let dishes build up. Which is weird because I'm generally so anal about that sort of stuff. I didn't make my bed. I left magazines and books strewn all over the floor. And I only cleaned the bathroom twice in six months. I had no-one to complain to. No-one to sulk about. No-one with whom I had a score to settle on the house-cleaning front by proving that when it came to washing and wiping, I was the winner.

If the window was left open, if the milk was put back empty, if the bin didn't get put out it was all my fault. That's some pretty heavy responsibility. If I left threatening notes declaring the resident of my premise a lazy, fiscally challenged, wine-swilling pig then it would only be me on the receiving end. I'm all for a bit of self-flagellation, but writing abusive letters to yourself is taking it a bit far. I think the odd angry text is okay. But longhand is just plain sad.

You have to be brave to live on your own. And resourceful. You have to kill your own spiders. And tune in your own telly. And change your own light bulbs. If I was left to living on my own I'd be in the dark surrounded by arachnids. If anything difficult, dangerous or disgusting needs to be done, like dealing with dog shit or feline hairballs or the unblocking of toilets, well that's my husband John's job. And I'm not being unfair. I am quite happy to do my share: flower arrangements, pillow fluffing and the odd spot of dusting. I've even been known to sew on the odd button.

There is a certain joy in living alone. I can definitely appreciate that. I think John fantasises about it regularly. Imagining the life he had, gloriously alone, that existed before me, where he could come home from work, grab a beer and watch the footy completely uninterrupted. He could water the garden in his underpants and smoke a cigarette and no-one would know. There was no-one standing on the back verandah nagging, 'What the fuck are you doing out there at this time of night and can I smell fire?'

While his life with me is definitely richer, it's become a lot busier. Perhaps at times for John a little too busy. In fact, if his life was a sausage, it would have bits of mince spewing out from the casing. It would be the sausage well pricked. I can see how he craves quiet time. I don't think there's been quiet time in our house for at least five years. It's chaos. Demands. Voices. Arrivals. Departures. Wiping. Cooking. Washing. Yelling. Crying. Laughing. In a house full of people you tend to melt into some sort of anomalous organism. There is no sense of individualism. You don't really ever get to choose what you want to eat or what you want to watch, you exist in a sea of compromise, so after a while you start to realise that what you want is what makes everyone else happy.

I think John would like some space to relax and read a book. Watch telly by himself. Sit and stare into space. Men seem to need to do that sort of thing a lot. Just staring. While holding their balls. It's how they think best.

I don't do alone time very well. It makes me anxious. It's too big. When I've been really stressed John has suggested I should go away on my own. But the thought of it fills me with fear. I find it creepy. Like I would just sit in a hotel thinking, 'Yippee, time on my own.' And then stare at the wall. Or watch cable. Or hit the mini bar. I don't like that. I relax so much better in my well-ordered world of chaos. I don't need space or time to discover myself. I'd rather lose myself in the confusion.

Eating alone is embarrassing. One of my girlfriends who has lived alone for many years treats it with melancholic amusement, posting photos of her delicious restaurant meals complete with sea view and glass of chilled sav blanc with captions such as 'Dinner for one' or 'Dining with the person I love'. She often tells me how weird it is when they put the table for one near a big group booking. Thank god for mobile phones. Now when you eat alone you can pretend you are checking your messages. In the past you chewed your food silently as you watched people with friends.

Cooking for one is the greatest challenge. It's not like you're going to knock out some culinary masterpiece for yourself. Cooking for yourself is like masturbating. If you can't get there under five minutes, you are going to lose interest and consider ordering out. Rice is always a winner. As is pasta. And of course toast. Thank god for toast. When you live alone, toast is your constant companion.

Toast and wanking, the simple salvation of those who live alone.

When I lived alone I ate far too much. I got a bit excited that there was no-one to witness ice-cream binges or late night chocolate hits. It only takes a week or two to realise that it's your arse that is the witness. And not always silent.

I'm not someone who has spent much time living alone. In fact it would be true to say that I tend to avoid it. I don't think it's that I don't like myself, it's just that I like myself more in the company of others. While I respect that living alone is a choice taken by some people, for some it may not be. For some it's possibly the consequence of poverty, or illness, or age or sadness.

What happens when a person who would love to live with others is suddenly alone? The death of a partner renders a person suddenly and inexplicably alone. I remember being a little girl hearing my mother weep and talk of the 'terrible loneliness' after my father died. I don't know how a person can ever be properly prepared for that. How do you accept such change with grace, rather than bitterness and regret? How do you adjust to the part of your brain used for petty nigglings like pointing out the irritations of your co-habiters now only being used to just sit and observe you. It must be like falling off the P&O cruise ship into the sea. No-one notices and the ship sails off. The thought of being old and alone with nothing but my thoughts frightens me. That's a place you go before you die. For some of us, purgatory might start on earth.

I wouldn't cope being alone. I would definitely start talking to myself. (I already do.) And answering back. People who live alone must always explain themselves, accept being excluded from invitations to couple dinner parties and set up with people's friends who also live alone. That would annoy me if I wasn't one of those couple people who actually treat people who live alone exactly like that.

I am no Greta Garbo. Being alone for too long makes me feel depressed. I actually like other people. I like the sense of them downstairs, or in the next room. It feels safe for me. Being alone feels unnatural. I think we're supposed to be in this big funky annoying community of children and old people and teenagers and goats … well, maybe not goats. It's supposed to be full of voices and noise and whingeing and laughing and screaming and eventually me freaking, 'If you don't stop that I'm leaving.' Then I storm outside.

And then there's me, sitting alone on the back step with a glass of wine gazing at the moon trying to steal back some 'me' time.

That's when I think of Thelma.

Sometimes it's very nice to be alone. Maybe the old girl had it right.

I WASH, THEREFORE I AM

Housework is what a woman does that nobody notices unless she hasn't done it.

Evan Esar

I do 30 loads of washing a week. I know because I did a washing audit. I was sick of complaining and getting nowhere. Men don't listen to the whingeing of women. In fact, evolution has ensured that men long ago developed a mechanism that allows them to turn off way before the nag gets a chance to hit fever pitch. They don't hear what you say. All they hear is the sound – something akin to a fire alarm going off when you're cooking – and all they want to do is get a broom and hit it. Or at least take the batteries out.

I wanted my husband to understand why I am such a nagging bitch and keep trying to have what he perceives as pedestrian conversations about my martyrdom that start like this: 'You have no idea how much I do around here …' It doesn't compute. He's a bloke. He needs numbers. Facts and figures. Numbers aren't emotional. They're just numbers. Numbers don't cry and throw tantrums. They just state the facts and go back to being numbers. I knew the only way to get my academically minded, science-brained husband to understand the cost of his clean underpants was to present a well researched laundry thesis that clearly shows the only reason he wears the pants is because I wash them.

It is important to me that my husband knows just how much of my precious time is occupied by an endlessly repetitive and deeply unsatisfying mundane task. His clean clothes simply turn up in the cupboard. His underpants miraculously clean themselves. Shirts return to hangers fresh and crisp and smelling of soap. Jeans are laundered and then fold themselves. Or so it would appear. Weary washerwomen know that no such magic exists. And so I sing the laundry fairies lament: 'Will my washing basket e'r be empti'd?'

The home is very often the place of toil. This place which is supposed to be our respite from the world of work, is ironically the place of even more work. In fact, I think people go to work to get away from the overwhelm of the work at home. Generally there's been a gender divide, where men 'went' to work and women stayed home to work. Thank god for the suffragettes and the feminists who came after them fighting for our right to go to work as well, so that we could leave the chains of home behind. Of course, they are always waiting for us on our return.

The home offers an unending list of tasks. Some will never be completed and some will be completed, only to reappear on the list to be completed all over again. There will be gutters requiring some sort of ladder and hose-assisted enema, books that need dusting, drawers that need sorting, cupboards stacked with sheets and towels in a mismatched array of chaos threatening an avalanche of linen at any moment, walls and windows that need grubby finger prints wiped off. While on that subject, can I ask how on earth walls get such disgusting black hand prints? Do people come straight from the garden to wipe their dirty mitts on my white walls? Have they been rolling in printers' ink? Do people actually lick the window glass when no-one else is watching? And must small insects hurl themselves at the glass and leave tiny corpses stuck in spots I can never reach?

Of course you could choose to leave it. To push things to the side. To decide not to care. To make peace with the clutter and choose to clear small spaces on the table to eat or do the crossword. To allocate a spare room for your ironing. And then close that door. Lock it. Fuck it, lose the key. Or perhaps the more spiritually enlightened task is to not iron at all. Although that means a lifetime in poly-blends or stretch knits. I can't do that. I have a panic attack just thinking about it. Doomed forever to be porridge in a body stocking. I like to wear cotton. It's so much more forgiving. And I like it crisp, not all scrunched up with the peg marks still in the shoulders. People judge you on shit like that. If I meet a woman with peg marks I know that's one lazy sister. Either that or she's evolved past the need for approval by judgmental cleaning obsessive bitches like me.

Some people don't care. They really don't. I find their lack of regard for order exciting – to me they are living on the edge and they haven't even left the couch. Actually, usually the reason they are on the edge is because they don't move from the couch. But it's stressful. I have friends like this and every time I visit all I want to do is wipe them down and do the dishes. I don't know why but disorder gets to me. I can't think in chaos. If my ceasarstone bench tops aren't cleared of dishes and wiped free of crumbs I have a small nervous breakdown. It's like the bench is my mind, and the crumbs are those aberrant nagging thoughts. If I wipe my bench, I wipe my mind. It's crazy, I know, but I see my connection to my home environment as an extension of my connection to my inner self. If I could spray Windex in my ear and get the same effect, I would.

You can't see your inner self. There is no physical representation of your internal monologues, fears and fantasies, paranoias, the persistent thoughts, the essence of the underlying you. So for me I put a picture to it. I am my house. When my house is in order, I am in order. And when it falls around my feet I am a screaming angry nutbag. It's very hard to explain this to my husband because to maintain the equilibrium on his internal sense of self he doesn't need jars facing the right way in the pantry.

I am hoping this is not just me. If it is, this book is less of an insightful attempt at humour and more of a cry for help. But I think that for a lot of us 'home' and 'self' are intrinsically linked. It was Jung who suggested that in the symbology of dreaming, when one dreams of houses, one is dreaming of one's inner self. My house dreams always involve a room I've never found before full of dead bodies and demons. I try to avoid any proper probing analysis and just accept that one of my charms is that I'm just a teensy bit disturbed. I like to think that everyone has a room where they keep their dead bodies.

I resent the hours of mindless housework I do every day, every week, every month. Every year. Resent is actually a rather mild word for how I feel sometimes. It enrages me. It fills me with violence. It makes me wonder if there's any space in that room for more dead bodies. I remember thinking that when I grew up and left home how I would be having fun all the time. I certainly didn't fantasise about changing sheets or pegging out underpants for other people who were busy having 'fun'.

There was this quite lovely period in my twenties where I used to allow myself a joint when I cleaned. It was amazing. In fact it was the only time I looked forward to housework. I'd spend all day engrossed in cleaning the toilet. Eight hours would float by and I would have scrubbed every tiny molecule to perfection. Painstakingly removed every lost pube lodged in the tile grout. It would sit there gleaming like a porcelain sculpture of serenity and whiteness. I would stand back and admire my work. And then someone would come in and piss on it.

In order to avoid complete nervous collapse I have come to believe that this daily grind is part of our modern mantra on the path to enlightenment. Vacuuming, scrubbing and wiping has become the contemporary version of 'chop wood and carry water'.

Clearly, no-one chops wood or carries water anymore. Unless you've opted for some sort of self-sustaining communal life and it's your job to take the bucket to the well and prepare the kindling. Then it's not just a metaphor. It's an entry on the to-do list.

Our daily rituals may have changed, but no matter how elevated we may become, existence still requires the completion of boring, unfulfilling and meaningless tasks that no-one really wants to do. For some reason I am yet to fathom, women very often are the gatekeepers of this realm.

In fact, I believe it's time to change the spiritual mantra to something like:

Before Enlightenment, pack and unpack dishwasher.

After Enlightenment, pack and unpack dishwasher.

Anyway, who needs enlightenment?

So back to my washing audit. I am at the washing line for a total weekly pegging out period of 300 minutes. It takes me another 300 minutes to take the washing off the line, fold it and put it away. That's 600 minutes of my week taken up with the cleansing of other people's clothes. That's ten hours. I don't want to appear unkind, but I am not just chopping wood and carrying water for me – I am doing it for six other people as well. That's a lot of wood and water that I carry for my husband, one son and four daughters.

The existence of the daily grind creates a nasty rash on the body politic that declares that individuals have the choice to be self-actualised, to live the dream, to meditate, mediate and masturbate themselves to other worldly greatness.

Every week I look around my house and I think, 'What is the point?' I wash dishes, I make beds, I pick up towels off the floor and hang them up. I take out the rubbish, I wipe down benches, I do the washing, I fold it and put it away, I vacuum. I clean the toilet, I mop, I dust. I clean the top of the fridge, I clean under the fridge, I clean the stove top, I empty crumbs from the toaster. For this very brief moment my house is clean. Order has been restored to the chaos. I breathe in this strange and transitory moment of peace and harmony before the inevitable slide back into mayhem. I make a cup of tea and sit at the table imagining how nice it would be to maintain this level of neatness on a daily basis. This perfectly controlled place where I can think in peace. This never happens.

I know the moment the fruit of my DNA step foot inside the house my carefully maintained sanctuary will be obliterated. Shoes discarded at the door, a rolled up rotting sock will leave its mate and find residence under the sideboard, a school bag will be dropped in the lounge with the zip open just enough to purge its contents onto the floor. Uniforms will be left inside out in crumpled balls on bedroom floors, DVD cases emptied with their discs sitting exposed on top of the TV cabinet. Milk on the bench. Slightly spilled. Unwashed cups in the sink. Toast crumbs return. The butter is left out. A towel makes its way back onto the floor. There's another fucking black smudgey handprint on the wall. Three hours after achieving order, disorder returns.

It drives me nuts. It wears me down. It's why women take valium. It's why women scream. Nag. Complain. Cry. Crawl into a fetal position under a doona and refuse to come out.

The other day I heard a startling piece of information on a BBC broadcast that was reporting on a bunch of physicists who'd met to discuss 'time'. Clearly they were able to do this because their wives were at home washing their shirts and undies allowing them the time to actually spend their life contemplating time.

Apparently we live in a state of continual entropy, meaning that it is a law of nature that everything moves to disorder. That's why your house gets messier rather than cleaner. That's why your car breaks down, and the grass gets long. Why everything eventually goes to shit. Thank god! The reason I struggle with housework is not because I am cleaning impaired, it's just that housework by its very nature goes against the basic principles of the universe. I am fatigued from battling the laws of science. I have often fantasised about living in a world where grass grows short and children's rooms become cleaner the longer you ignore them. The Benjamin Button effect on everything.

Then I realised, in one profound dishwasher unpacking epiphany, that this meaningless task, this dreary ritual that has me on my knees three times a day, is life. Life is not all about choice. Sometimes it's about subjugating one's own desires and ego at the service of the mundane. The endless grind of daily rituals and chores is the anvil that anchors my ego to the ground, that stops me floating skywards, becoming puffed up and unbearable. There is strange magic in the boring ordinary places we must inhabit. There are many people who would benefit from doing 30 loads of washing a week. I have often wondered when James Packer last washed his underpants himself.

These are the things that pass through my mind while vacuuming. These are the times were I have found I can engage in the monk-like art of sideways thinking. Allowing the mind to wander as the body engages in physical activity is easier and more productive than you'd think, and it's surprisingly creative. Once I stopped being angry and allowed my mind to unravel, I found that I could clean and meditate at the same time. It's so much easier to dust hard to reach spots when you can levitate.

I have been contemplating running classes called 'Using Your Hills Hoist to Unlock your Stream of Consciousness'. A person cannot be creatively, fabulously productive all the time. There are many hours of the day when a person merely needs to surrender to existence, to fall into the hum of life. To calm the mind and those constant anxious demands for greater output, more money, more ideas. My daily grind is about discipline. It's about embracing a routine that allows me the space to create. In fact, if I were to analyse my creative outputs, I would have to admit that the busier I have become the more prolific my output.

How can this make sense? How is it that at age 27, when I was at my peak physical fitness, when I had left my 'day job' to pursue my career as a comedian and writer, that I virtually got nothing done? I shared a house, so my responsibilities were few. I never managed to really do anything. I think I wrote a few paragraphs and then threw them away because they were just one long rambling whinge about how no-one really understood me. I couldn't focus. I couldn't think. I had no discipline. I had so much time on my hands it crippled me. I had no understanding of the importance of the NOW because I had so much of it.

Now at 46, with five children ranging from 5 to 19, a giant six-bedroom house, a massive mortgage, a delightful husband

and a social network of friends and family that I must constantly juggle, I find myself at my peak creativity.

I schedule everything, including having a poo. I'm not kidding. There was this one time I didn't schedule it and by day 4, I suddenly realised the urgent need for serious 'downtime'. I make lists. Lists of lists of lists. I make a plan of what I must achieve each week, kind of like a budget, and when an hour or two becomes available, I take it. I don't procrastinate, I don't have time. Procrastination is for people with too little to do. It's a luxury for the underwhelmed. I generally get things done because I do them. I don't think too much about it.

So strangely, I live a very busy, very productive, very rich, very hard-working life. I realise that I am happiest in this paradoxically well-organised tsunami of creative energy because for me, creativity is like a bottomless abyss, and the demands of my life ensure that I don't ever entirely fall in. I can't afford to, there's always a bin to put out, a lunch to make or a dishwasher to unpack.

It was only recently when seeing a psychiatrist for one of my kids and I was giving a detailed family history that he pointed out, 'So you have OCD.' I was a bit shocked. It had never occurred to me that I might have some sort of obsessive disorder. But there was some intrusive thinking as a child, counting, hand washing, and I was a bit of a relentless over-achiever. After the initial slump when I realised I was a little bit crazy, I appreciated the upside to mental illness. My OCD and my strange ability to obsess on seemingly meaningless details had allowed me a strange sort of focus.

And so it has been true. The bigger, the busier, the more full-on my life has become, the bigger, busier and more productive I have become. I have never believed children were an excuse for me not to be productive. In fact, they were a reason why I had to be. My kids have always been creative touchstones, exposing me to ideas and challenges that I might have otherwise missed. Of course the grind still grinds. I am just a hunk of parmesan on life's big grater.

No matter how philosophical I can become about the merits of hard work, about the Joy of Vac, there's also no way in hell I'll ever give up whingeing about it! Of course, I'd never really let anyone else do it. As if they'd do it properly! But I do realise, in some strange sort of way, that my creativity is somehow intrinsically linked to all those things I do every day that no-one will ever see. The boring, mindless meaningless shit that somehow keeps me sane.

Even Einstein had to clean his toilet. Or at least his wife did.

THE HOUSE THAT JACK (AND JILL) BUILT

Cheops' Law: Nothing ever gets built on schedule or within budget.

Robert A Heinlein, *Time Enough for Love*

*P*eople building a house for the first time should sit down and read the story of *The Three Little Pigs*. And I don't mean skim read it, I mean REALLY read it! This isn't just a story warning about the dangers of wolves; this is a roadmap for initiates new to the building game and prepares we little piggies for encounters with the lazy, the opportunistic and the downright predatory. The three little pigs pose a perplexing riddle: when little piggies venture out into the world, just who and with what, are they going to build their precious home? And how do you recognise a big bad wolf along the way? I remember reading a quote by Angela Carter in her contemporary retelling of *Little Red Riding Hood* that a person who is 'dodgy' isn't always visible …' and the worst kind of men (sorry blokes but tradies and builders are generally blokes) 'are the ones that are hairy on the inside.' That has always given me the creeps and has served as a reminder to be wary of shysters.

I have no radar for con men or bullshit artists, which made the whole building process terrifying. Everyone seems really nice to me. I am very trusting. I think it's because I'm one of those 'what you see is what you get' type people so being an idiot, I assume that everyone else is just like me. I'm also plagued with a nasty case of 'ethics' which is probably why I've ended up broke. Sometimes I wish I could reach inside and smash that bloody moral compass. It's such a conundrum, to be so moral and so shallow, both at the same time.

I'm not saying that the building process is full of criminals and you are going to be ripped off. Actually, I am. Because I think if you approach the whole process with suspicion, you end up being a lot less disappointed in people and as a bonus, you also end up with that lovely pious feeling that I call, 'See, I was right'. And if it turns out you were wrong, it's a wonderful moment for reinstating your belief in humanity.

Building a house is an enormous exercise of trust. And it's a lot of money. You have to trust that it's not going to fall around your ears and that the 2D plans are going to translate to 3D. It's a massive exercise in faith when you consider you are basically paying for a house that doesn't yet exist, built by strangers, that will have you enslaved to the bank for the next 30 years.

Although the sales pitch would have you believe that people in the building industry are there solely to build your dreams, it becomes pretty evident early on in the process that they are there to build your dreams, *but at significant profit to themselves.* Which makes sense. Dreams cost money. And random acts of altruism don't happen in the building industry. The price of your dream pays their wage so they can go have a crack at their dream. Corners that can be cut will be cut, where cheaper materials can be substituted, they will be substituted, and anything you don't understand or couldn't do yourself will always cost a bomb. Yes, in the supplying of your dream, sometimes you get a few nightmares.

I loved building our house. In fact I would love to do it again. Just to have another shot making stressful decisions and getting a higher ratio of good results to crap results. For a first timer I think I did okay, but there were certainly a few areas where I dropped the ball.

It seems ludicrous to be losing sleep over choosing stuff that you previously had never noticed or didn't know the name of, but now had you in an insomniac stupor worrying, 'Did I choose the right cornices?'

In my pre-house building incarnation I did not know what a cornice was. Cornice sounds like the less attractive sister of Beatrice. Basically a cornice is the bit that joins your wall to your ceiling. It's one of the thousands of choices you make when you are building. When you buy a house, you basically get the cornices you are given, a choice laboured over by another cornice-perplexed woman in another time. Christ, I've only just located the G spot. Now I need to find my cornice.

Suddenly everywhere I went all I looked at were the cornices. Did I want something busy, heritage, chunky, discreet? From what I can tell, the choices could be renamed 'dull' 'duller' or 'even duller still'. Somewhere someone had a job making dull as shit mouldings. At a dinner party someone would ask, 'Marjorie, what do you do?'

'Oh,' Marjorie would reply, 'I do the admin for a company that manufactures cornices.'

Fucking hell, Marjorie. Was that your dream job? Was that the pinnacle you strived for? The edge that you pushed yourself towards in your attempt to navigate the road less travelled? As a schoolgirl did the margins of all your notebooks contain doodlings of cornice designs? Did you harbour a secret dream to go out there and change the world one cornice at a time? To create unique, contemporary, historical cornices? Or maybe a cornice that would become an instant talking point? Like a cornice with a more Roman feel, with the wall being joined to the ceiling with the help of giant carved phalluses. If that had been in the catalogue, I would have chosen that. The cock cornice. It wasn't. I didn't know what I wanted. I didn't know how a person's life could be affected by bad cornices so I went for something plain and uninspiring. Like Marjorie did.

The cornice wasn't the only new word to make its way into my home owners glossary. Just the other day I found out there is a 'coping guy'. I was at Outdoor Leisure Fucking World or some colossal load of horse manure like that, chatting to the pool 'consultant' and he said, 'We'll send over the coping guy.'

I was shocked. I've had five kids to three different blokes and only now they tell me there's a coping guy. Some sort of super dude who can handle the shit demanding, difficult and obstreperous women like me dish out on a daily basis. I'm up for the challenge. I reckon I could bust coping guy's arse in a week. Just wait coping guy, in no time at all you'll be covered in baby sick, clutching your fat gut while opening the letter of demand from the credit card company screaming, 'I can't cope! I can't cope!'

I had it wrong. Apparently the coping guy does the little bit of tile around the pool. For some bizarre reason they call that coping. I would have called it tiling. Clearly men don't stay at home with the kids because in my books, that is coping. Tile around the pool is tiling. Anyway I am happy to say I managed to break the coping guy in just one day. The people at the Leisure Centre told me it was a record. He found it unreasonable to be asked to perform 'coping' in the absence of a pool. Minor bloody details, mate. Can't you see I'm installing the perimeter of the pool in my effort to manifest the contents? Some tradies have no bloody imagination and are totally out of touch with their inner wild woman. I lent him *Women Who Run With Wolves* as I reckon a man who spends his life decorating edges should get to know a few of his own.

This hyper-vigilant attention to nothing turned me into Rainwoman. Everywhere I went I paid close attention to door handles, light switches, fascia, paving stones, bench tops and taps. It was as if a whole new world of fittings opened up. One day I was at a friend's house and I accidentally said out loud, 'I don't like your taps.' My friend looked at me confused, but then we both realised I'd verbalised a thought that couldn't be retrieved. It was in the public domain and now I had to run with it.

'No offence,' (this is the preamble meant to disarm offensive statements), 'but I don't like your taps.' My friend had only just built her house and I'd come over and insulted her taps. All my raving of, 'Love your deck, wow look at the tiles! Your ensuite is amazing,' meant nothing after I dissed her plumbing. I don't think she really likes me anymore, which is okay because I really don't like her taps. I remember looking at her taps and thinking, 'Wow, if you can choose a tap like that, then I guess I don't really know you.'

My tap sensitivity led me to long nights googling 'taps'. It's done all manner of strange things to the algorithm that generates advertising on my Facebook page. Thanks to my searches, it would appear that I am a target market for bathroom fittings, handbags and anal beads. I promise I didn't search anal beads, well, not on the same night as the taps at least.

Being a novice at house building, it had never occurred to me that someone actually chose all that shit, piece by flipping piece. When you live in a house where all the choices have already been made, you just accept that's the way things are. Unless you embark on some sort of major reno, most of us learn to live with other people's choices. While you may hate the colour of the walls, or the bathroom tiles and the strange windows that don't open properly, the fact is that some other idiot chose them, not you. It was in the building process that it dawned on me that now my husband and I were the idiots making the choices.

This was my opportunity to create a house that would have family and friends gasping. As they proclaim, 'Wow! I mean WOW!' they are actually thinking, 'Wow, what the fuck? I mean what kind of idiot would choose a cornice without a cock in it?' Pre-house building I used to worry that I was too fat for my skinny jeans. Now I fall asleep at night worrying that my deck doesn't match my support beams. Which I guess is the architectural equivalent of my chubby white muffin top.

The whole building process took us three and a half years. For a woman who has lived her life in the grip of instant gratification, this was torture. The building itself took only six months, but the subdivisions and the council approvals dragged on for a staggering 1120 days. For 1120 nights all I could think about was my dream house. What I would build. Who would build it. In my mind I built 1120 houses. I walked through the rooms. I installed giant cantilevered decks over infinity pools that actually went on for infinity. When you are in the visioning process, it seems stupid to limit your vision with something as trivial as a budget. There's nothing more boring than having someone turn up mid-fantasy to deliver the unwelcome news, 'I am sorry Mandy, but the 20-metre square bathroom with the polished concrete floors and the glass wall looking into the rainforest is not going to work because, for a start, you can barely afford a 12-metre square room and you're living in the suburbs, not the Daintree.'

The house I built in my imagination is almost as splendid as the life I imagined living inside of it. You see, it's not just about the actual building. I was visioning an amazing set design for my new amazing life. Of course in this new amazing life, sitting on my new amazing couch in my new amazing lounge/family room, I would be wearing white jeans and have super white teeth, because I would be amazing too. I wouldn't be fat in this house. No, I would drop that 20 kilos that has gravitated to my gut and thighs and I would be skinny. Because only skinny women live in beautiful houses and wear white jeans – they live lives compatible with white jeans. In my mind I built the perfect white jean life. Then I imagine someone breaks in and stabs me and splatters blood on my jeans and my couch and my perfect white dream looks like a scene from *Carrie*.

Unlike me, my husband is a realist. My visioning process terrified him. My sense of dimension was more akin to a Sheraton lobby than a modest suburban dwelling, and as my scrapbook started filling with pictures of houses that we would never build, John thought it was time I made contact with our financial limitations. When we had the first conversation I started crying because I thought he was intentionally deflating my dream house. He'd got out his big pin of pragmatic realism and pricked my puffy paradise.

John then took me for a drive to a housing estate and started pointing at houses that we might actually be able to build. It wasn't as bad as I had thought. I had fears he was going to force me into an AV Jennings brick and tile and I was ready to threaten him with bout of depression so long-lasting he would end up wishing he hadn't been such a tightarse. Once I'd stopped sulking about losing my mansion, it occurred to me that a modest dream was better than no dream at all. So I got involved. I started noticing things about people's houses that I had never noticed before. We'd be driving along and I'd shout, 'Stop John, back it up, I have to get a photo of that fence.' It must be pretty creepy going out for your morning jog only to discover a woman leaning out the car taking photographs of your front yard. I actually yelled out to one bloke who looked like he was going to come out and punch me, 'Don't worry, I'm not stalking. This is for my scrapbook!'

On one occasion I liked a fence so much I knocked on the front door to ask about it. The kid that answered gave me the 'crazy lady' look kids reserve for adults they find unnerving. 'Mum, there's a big lady at the door who likes our fence.'

Driving around looking at people's houses was starting to feel a bit predatory, and I have to admit it was very frustrating. I was rarely let inside. I'd have to get a glimpse of kitchen layouts from the window. There was even a point when I considered joining the Jehovah Witness crew on the off-chance someone might invite me in and I'd get to have a good look around.

In order to imagine what I wanted in my house, I needed to see it. A few lines with some measurements suggesting dimension on a piece of paper don't mean anything to me. I need to walk around and get the feel of a room. To me, architecture is about what a place feels like when you are in it. Where I would put my couch. Or my bed. Or where I would drink my tea. While I can imagine the difference between a 15-foot ceiling and a 8-foot one, its not until you walk into a space that you really feel the difference. I am 6-foot, so the prospect of living in an 8-foot room with a ceiling fan is terrifying. It's the stuff that fuels dreams of domestic decapitation. All I'd have to do is reach up to put my bra on and I'm the next Jack Newton.

Some people are very helpful. For instance, someone who has just built a home is very, very useful, especially if they are prepared to share some of the tricks of the trade by way of a few hot tips, especially in the 'try and avoid' category. Although it would be my advice to visit someone a year after they've moved in so you can get a real feel about how their choices stacked up with a bit of wear and tear. Are tiles cold to live on? Does the scraping of metal legs of a chair drive you nuts on polished concrete? Do you regret not building the vacuum unit into the wall? (I mean, how do you get your penis into that?) Are all ceiling fans ugly? Can you live without them? What is the exact number of downlights that start to make your house look like an art gallery or a lighting showroom? Is air conditioning the only way to combat global warming? If I install a giant free-standing bath, will I actually use it? How many toilets is too many toilets? What is the best towel rack? (A friend says 'heated' which you will use seven times before the electricity bill comes in.) Does anyone use media rooms or do they just become the dark stinking airless armpit of the house? And just how small can I get away with making the children's rooms to gain myself some space on the 'parents' retreat'?

I've always loved the term 'parents' retreat', like it's possible to actually go somewhere in the house to escape the chaos and the reality of having blood-sucking dependents. I guess when there's a bunch of them in the downstairs rumpus pulling bongs and playing *Grand Theft Auto*, then you are going to want somewhere to curl up in the foetal position rocking back and forth crying, 'What have I done wrong? What have I done?'

It's the same perplexing terror when it comes to building, the self-doubt is endless, and the in-depth conversations between the 'just built' and the 'soon to build' are engrossing. Of course, if you are in neither of these categories and you are a dinner party guest, then you may consider stabbing yourself in the eye with a fork for some sort of topic decoy or at the very least some short-term amusement.

People building houses are very, very boring. That brain that used to deliberate on world politics and issues of planetary and humanitarian concern, is now primarily occupied with shallow anxieties such as 'will a lime green splashback in the kitchen be too much?' I thought about that for six months. As it turns out, it was worth the night terrors. I may have missed my best friend's birthday, Father's Day and worming the kids, but the kitchen is fucking perfect.

One of our 'interior consultants' gave us some good advice on colour choice. 'Don't be scared about making more flamboyant choices. Everything dates. Even white.' I got the feeling that she told people what they wanted to hear because brown laminex and purple tiles, while a glorious reminder of the 70s with a contemporary retro twist, has a use-by date of about two weeks.

While white may be a bit boring, I guess it does give you the option to add your own changing splash of colour, even if it is just the vibrant red of the blood pooling on the tiles after you've murdered the interior consultant.

It took me ages to settle on a house design that I liked. It was like choosing a husband: I didn't trust myself. I had to go and consider everything just so that I could eliminate it, thus reinforcing whatever choice I was to make. John and I embarked on perhaps the most time-consuming and mindless yet integral part of the house-building journey: visiting display homes.

Display homes, for those unfamiliar with this part of the 'window shopping' house market, are supplied as examples of excellence for plebs like us who couldn't afford an architect. These houses are fully fitted out by the interior consultants, are neatly landscaped and represent the perfect dream home. It's perfect, of course, because no-one has ever lived there. The minute one greasy child hand opens the fridge the gloss starts to dull and the dream of the perfect Barbie house dies.

Oh and what they also forget to tell you is that the house you are looking at is for display only. You won't be able to afford that, it's not even in the range. Like some sort of elaborate rat trap set with fancy cheese. It's not until you feel the snap of the wire on the back of your neck that you realise you've been done. John and I visited about 100 display homes in a 400-kilometre radius. It was ridiculous. You see, at first we thought we were looking at what we could actually buy. But these were 'display', not real homes. The real homes were in the new development ghettos and didn't look anything like these homes. It would be far less disappointing if they had put a sign out the front of a display village that read, 'By all means have a look and fantasise that one day this will be yours, but on that budget, nothing you build will ever look like this … dickhead!'

I reckon you could use the viewing of display homes as some sort of torture. I'd call it 'death by display'. After a while they all look the same. Some bloke or woman working for the building company in the garage pretending to be remotely interested and lines of zombies trailing in and out of the rooms marvelling at the wonder of the walk-in wardrobes, plush velvet cinema/media rooms and amazing indoor/outdoor entertaining areas.

Every house we went into had this amazing incorporation of inside and out. It was like finally house designers had cottoned on to the balmy Queensland/ northern NSW climate and realised that for most of the year, we're sweating our tits off. So instead of boxing us in to our neat little housing Tupperware, they create these kitchen/dining/barbeque/ leisure areas that courtesy of stacker doors, seem to run into each other. It's a new world order outlawing the previous design apartheid that delineated two zones: inside and outside. Now the inside goes outside and the outside feels like inside. It's like living in the yard.

I loved these areas. I wanted one. I wanted to be cooking in my luxurious MasterChef appointed kitchen while chatting to my husband reading the paper in the outside leisure area. This went well beyond my previous dream of a banana lounge on the back porch. I am talking wood-fired frickin' pizza oven, a stainless steel fully plumbed outdoor kitchen, and a shiny $5000 barbeque with a casual setting for 12 surrounded by Italian day beds, succulent vertical gardens, a massive pool and of course tinkling water feature that made me want to piss my pants 24 hours a day. Who cares if it makes me incontinent, imagine the ambience! I'd be more than happy to wear a panty liner for the privilege!

My kids loved going to display homes. They imagined every display home was ours. They'd run through the house and jump on the beds going 'this one is mine' or they'd lie on the lounge, or test the toilet with a poo. (You aren't supposed to poo in display homes. I told my youngest not to flush – I was worried about being caught – and instead we left a 'display' poo, which after all seemed entirely appropriate).

At first I'd try and shush the children. Tell them not to touch. Don't be so loud. Don't touch the balls. All display homes have balls. It's like some interior decorating convention – all tables must have a bowl as a centerpiece and in the absence of real life (being fruit) there are designer balls. Some ceramic, glass, wood, marble. You name it, there's a ball in a bowl somewhere in a display home made out of it. For my youngest, display homes were an opportunity to throw balls. We may have broken the odd ball, and I made it a game to pocket a ball from every bowl. Now I have more balls than the Australian Cricket team.

After about 40 houses I didn't give a shit about keeping my family under control. In fact I found the whole process so deceptive I felt this subversive desire to undermine the process and when it came to the kid's conduct, I was guilty on more than one occasion of encouraging anarchy. Towards the end I even developed the Display House Challenge, and while I never managed to work up the courage to have sex with my husband in the display home master bedroom, one day we did all strip off down to our undies and jump in the pool.

It was my husband's crack in the air naked bomb dive that invoked the ire of the chap in the garage who then demanded we leave. Fuck him. I took two of his stupid balls.

After six months of display home reconnaissance I confided in John that I liked the first one best. I was sitting in the front seat juggling my new balls when I delivered the news he'd been waiting for. 'I like the first house best.'

If I was to be honest it was at about house 18 that I realised that all the houses we looked at were built on a flat block. Our block was on a steep ridge overlooking a mountain. Only the first company were prepared to vary their designs to suit us and build into the hill. I assured John that the last 23 weekends had not been wasted. It was important to see the other 99 houses just to be sure.

When you are designing your home you not only have to think about your family situation now, you have to imagine it into the future. Who will leave? Who will get pregnant young and stay? Whose parents will need to live in the granny flat? Shit, we don't have a granny flat. Never mind, we'll whack a shower and bathroom in the garage, they'll never know the difference. Besides it saves on furniture – they can sleep in the car.

Our consideration was vast. Five children ranging from three to 17, both John and I needed home offices, I wanted to have an art studio and of course there is the necessary inclusion of the sex dungeon. Somewhere alongside the hair-removing, vodka-drinking and Kanye-listening lifestyle of the teenage girls I wanted an adolescent-free sanctuary to safeguard the innocence of my youngest two. Frankly, I don't know why I bothered.

Most houses are designed with the nuclear family of two parents and two or three children. Step-families like ours are much more challenging, and are not catered for in the display villages. Our family structure required a more elaborate floor plan than three bedrooms, a bathroom and a kitchen. You have to consider the importance of good insulation when one of the 18-year-olds may be having sex with her boyfriend downstairs, while upstairs someone is watching *Play School*. Ergh. I know. I hate *Play School*.

I wanted everything bigger. Ceilings, rooms, verandahs, windows, bathrooms. My husband kept saying smaller. Smaller is cheaper. Smaller is in our budget. Smaller is sustainable. Smaller is for losers. 'But I'm shallow,' I cried. 'I want big.' It didn't matter how much I begged, my husband insisted we stick to budget, that I take my giant white-jean dream and shrink it down to size. The constantly reducing dimensions had me convinced we were building a Lego house. In the end I got a front deck, albeit not 20 metres x 30 metres but a modest 4 x 4 which still allows me to go outside and look down at the neighbours. Of course had it wrapped around I could have got a whole lot more gloating in. The back deck is slightly more substantial, and eventually when we get the money to finish the deck downstairs that will lead to the infinity pool … that deck will be awesome.

You see, there's something I learnt about building. It opens the door to a world full of wanting and once you go there, you never frickin' finish.

Dream on.

ALMOST HOME

When I was a kid my parents moved a lot,
but I always found them.

Rodney Dangerfield

*T*he problem with moving into a new house is that everything is perfect. Too perfect. Floors are sparkling, tile grout is grime free, windows are glistening, eaves are free of cobwebs and walls have not been bumped, chipped or smeared with dirty fingers.

A house is never as clean as the day you first step foot in it and ruin it with your existence. From day one it's just a downhill slide into filth.

As a woman with definite OCD tendencies, the concept of deterioration perplexed me. I wanted to keep my new house feeling like a new house for as long as I could. At one point I even considered keeping it empty, staying in our rental and just popping by to visit our gleaming tribute to perfection. Of course this was never going to happen, we were all busting at the seams to make our mark, so I had a plan. Having never lived in a new home or even my 'own' home before, there was no way I was going to let this place slip into the lacklustre hovels that my rentals all eventually became.

And let me qualify something for landlords on behalf of tenants everywhere. Even the best of us lose interest in cleaning your house week after week. It just seems pointless busting your arse to maintain someone else's property. Of course if I rented my house I would expect people to keep it to my standard, but having been a renter most of my life, I now know that is never going to happen.

As a renter I would always start off with great intentions. I'd scrub the floors, bleach the walls, weed the garden. Six months later the garden looks like a bonsai Amazon and I'm marvelling at the mushrooms growing in the tile grout, reticent to remove them in case they are habitat for bathroom fairies. In most cases rental properties are fitted with the cheapest appliances, the shittiest fittings, the nastiest carpet. I mean, why would you put top quality product into a rental? Here is the conundrum. Cheap and nasty shit deteriorates a lot faster than expensive quality shit. So when you get your property returned, chances are cheap and nasty shit will need to be replaced with more cheap and nasty shit. Nearly every landlord I've ever had has always had this slightly shocked look that the house they leased five years before doesn't look quite the same. 'It's called wear and tear,' I politely reminded a previous landlord. 'You may have painted it when we moved in, but over half a decade has passed. I suggest you google "entropy" and get back to me with my bond.'

While the comfort or aesthetic environment of your tenant may not be your primary concern, it should be stated that tenants who are treated to generous and benevolent landlords tend to maintain the rental property at a much more impressive level than tenants who have to deal with stingy arseholes. When you've given up the fight with the rat living in the oven and you've asked 120 times for a replacement appliance only to be told 'no', you tend to develop a less than positive attitude towards household maintenance. Let's just say the 'laissez-faire' approach of the landlord is mirrored in the even more laissez-faire approach of the tenant.

It's depressing cleaning a house that is falling around your ears and not having the power that comes with ownership to repair the broken taps, busted light fittings or leaks in the roof. Sometimes all a woman can do is open a bottle of wine and let the alcohol soften the edges.

I once lived in a house that had so many leaks in the roof that when it rained, we had to sit under umbrellas on the couch to watch the telly. Once an area of the roof got so soggy a possum actually fell through. For the next few days we were treated to an indoor wildlife park with three fluffy tails swinging playfully in the corner of my bedroom. They disappeared after an ugly scuffle a few nights later, and the next day instead of a fluffy possum tail, a python tail hung in its place. This wasn't the only snake on the property. There was a nest of baby browns under the front steps. I'd become accustomed to the odd snake shooting out as I went to the outside laundry. Previously I had a fear of snakes, but I soon found out I had a bigger fear of losing control of my washing basket. I'd rather face a snake than put off a load.

I trained the kids to bang on the steps a few times before they went outside. I don't think the kids went out there alone ever. They were terrified of the backyard, and part of me kind of enjoyed their fear. My daughter Zoe had a habit of threatening to run away if she didn't get her own way. It was comforting to know she was too afraid of leaving the house to make a run for it.

If the kids did go outside they made sure they were wearing jeans, shoes and carried a stick. They would walk around asking things like, 'Mum, did I just stand on a snake?' Sometimes, just to be a bitch I'd say, 'I don't think so. The thing is with snakes they can bite you and you'd never know. Just feels like a twig brushing against your leg.' Then they would start crying and beg to be escorted inside to the safety of violence on TV and paedophiles posing as teenagers on Facebook. That kind of danger they can negotiate. Unseen terrors of twigs that could be snakes was the stuff of nightmares. Besides, we are not outdoorsy people. Sure I like nature, but generally I like to look at it from a chair on my deck or while enjoying the dulcet tones of David Attenborough.

As well as the snake in the roof and the ones under the back stairs, we also had one above the front step. An exposed piece of timber in the eaves housed a night tiger that would occasionally greet you with full eye-to-eye contact as you were struggling to get the key in the lock. There was no landing or flat area to rest your bag while you fumbled for the keys. Just a wobbly top step. The first time I got eyeballed by that snake I literally fell backwards down twelve stairs. I swear that snake literally pissed itself. 'Hss hss hss.' It laughed like a chain smoker with last-stage emphysema.

That house cured my fear of snakes. When you are living in the snake pit, you have to make friends with your enemy. I used to try and calm the children's anxieties with 'at least we know where they are. The snakes you have to worry about are the ones you can't see.' That's true. I meant it more as a metaphor for dangers in life, rather than an actual wildlife warning, but the kids all now have a catatonic fear of snakes. Especially the ones that aren't there.

That house was on a main road. It had giant curtainless windows facing the street. In fact, it was opposite what is commonly known as 'the hitching tree'. This was a large fig tree on a traffic island with a bench seat underneath. People would sit there for hours waiting for a lift.

From my desk in the front room I witnessed drug deals, the odd biffo, crying, swearing and once a couple fucking. It was a bit creepy. My teenager daughter came running to me one night freaked out because she was in her room putting on her bra when she heard a voice from outside at the hitching tree yell out, 'Nice tits!' I rushed into her room and took off my top. That's one way to silence a heckler.

Living in the full view of passersby is a bit like being on a reality TV show. You don't need cameras when the viewers are outside. This is real life streaming from a window near you. I had to cover every window with fabric. It was like living inside a velvet box. So I was looking forward to a new house, one without blockout curtains, snakes and perverts looking at your tits.

Moving into our gorgeous brand-new house offered a point of change for all of us. I declared that this would be a new era in my history of housekeeping. Never again would I lose control of our stuff. I'd lost the battle at our rental. Every square centimetre of that house was filled with stuff. Stuff on stuff. Stuff under stuff. Stuff stuffed into stuff. Stuff on cupboards. Stuff in cupboards. Stuff wedged behind cupboards. Stuff under beds. Stuff behind doors. Stuff under the house. Stuff in the roof. Stuff on the verandah. I had stuffed so much stuff into that place it was like living in an episode of serial hoarders. Although I should add that most of the stuff was brand-new, flat-packed stuff destined for The New House. I had decided that nothing from the old house would go to the new house. And nothing destined for the new house was to be touched in the old house. I hadn't factored in the three-year wait and my growing shopping addiction.

I felt like a big fat caterpillar weaving a cocoon. When I burst forth as the white-jeaned butterfly, it would be on a white leather couch in my new white leather, new furniture life. I started to hate everything I owned as it represented my old life, and set about replacing it. Stashed around the 'old house' were new dinner sets, new towels, new sheets, expensive new cookware, new glasses, new cups, new beds, new bedside tables, new lamps, an Italian toaster and kettle, designer linen, an eight-seater dining room setting, new outdoor furniture ... I wasn't just looking forward to moving into the new house, I was excited about busting out the new gear, about finally being able to have a shower and dry myself with a towel that didn't feel like a loofer.

When the time came to clear out the old house it was epic. Moving what I'd decided to keep was relatively simple – it was flat packed in boxes under the house. Everything going to the new house had been boxed and ready for years. Now I was in for the real test for anyone committed to moving on: letting go. I had set myself a challenge to make my life easier by eradicating clutter. It meant letting go of most of the things I'd been hanging onto for the last two decades. This was a challenge. Although I have found it is much easier to throw out the things that your husband feels sentimental about than your own.

My husband John is sentimental about everything. The only thing standing between me and my clutter-free life was John. John loves horrible shit. I can't believe I love a man with such bad taste. We had some of our biggest fights around me trying to force him to let go of the boxes of weird stuff that he'd become attached to. He refused to so I sulked and when that didn't work, I re-packed his sentimental shit into boxes which I marked 'sentimental shit'. If there is ever a flood I will make sure they are stored low enough to be ruined.

This is an inventory of some of the things in John's sentimental shit box. An old plastic coca-cola bottle. He was mortified when he caught me binning it and shrieked, 'That's my special coke bottle.' Bullshit. Who has a 'special coke bottle'? Apparently John does. It's the coke bottle that he used to drink water out of on fishing trips with his mates. I imagine this was from the era where

I didn't exist and thus the empty plastic bottle is imbued with spiritual significance. I started wondering what was next? The special sock he used to wank into as a teenager?

There was his Rabbitoh's flag, which he'd once tried to hang in our bedroom. I was conceived in the back seat of a car after Dad won his football grand final – I am not sleeping under a footy flag. My inner bogan is so well formed I am at risk of it taking my outer middle class bitch hostage any day now. Then there were his football jerseys. Every jersey he'd ever worn, in fact. Considering he'd played football until he was 49 it was a serious stockpile of jerseys. I joked 'Hmm they'll look nice framed up for the lounge room'. John thought it was a great idea.

There were also the usual suspects: photographs, letters and of course the drawings and craft constructions of his daughter Rachel. I don't think he has thrown out a single thing she's given him. When it comes to my kids getting crafty I am ruthless. I keep nothing. Today's pasta necklace is in tomorrow's bin. Of course, if its particularly amazing I'll keep it for what seems the appropriate length of time before it hits the skids. I remember being caught by Zoe throwing out her prize-winning Harry Potter diorama. Shit, this could be scarring. I reversed out of that tight corner like a champ. 'Had a snake living in it Zoe, but I can keep it if you want.' She begged me to throw it out. Game, set and match to Mummy.

There were plastic bottles with beads stuck to them, drawings, bits of tin with crepe paper, toilet rolls taped to toilet rolls in make-shift binoculars. The craft booty was unbelievable. I could understand keeping this if your child had died, but even then I think there would come a point when the utilitarian in you would go, 'I'll take a photo,' and be done with it. John would not relent. Even when I got Rachel to come in to bat on the 'take a photo Dad' he wouldn't budge. No, he'll be going to his grave with his toilet roll binoculars.

This was only the beginning of our de-cluttering conflicts. While John eventually acquiesced to my desire to purge our life of the past and move valiantly into a future unmarred by bits of furniture from our numerous previous relationships, there were some items that he went into battle hard for. Like the colonial-style dresser made from corrugated iron and railway sleepers. It was so ugly I used to gag every time I walked past it. I was tempted to burn it to the ground and then say to John, 'You wouldn't believe it, the dresser caught fire today – in a freak accident! I accidentally poured petrol over it and then lit it. By accident!' There were these conversations that we would have when John would try and convince me that some hideous old wooden relic was worth a lot of money. I remember thinking, yes it is, I would pay thousands to get rid of it!

Purging the past from the old house was cathartic. There were still boxes under the house from my previous marriage. It took something like 20 trips to the tip and four garage sales to get rid of this enormous tide of broken chairs, couches, beds, cupboards, old toys, paintings, record players, tents, Rabbitoh's flags ...

The garage sale has become a cultural phenomenon. Every weekend someone in your street decides to empty the unwanted contents of their life onto the front lawn in the vain hope that passersby will be wooed by their waste. They hope that their trash will become someone else's treasure. Somewhere out there exists a person who can love the unlovable. Especially when it's a bargain.

A garage sale is very revealing. It's a consumerist strip tease. You can tell a lot about a person by what they don't want. It's like a taste audit. The chipped vase, the unwanted CD collection, the decrepit sideboard all somehow signify the person you once were. Your discarded possessions are the remnants of an era you lived in, of a body that you'll never reclaim, or a sad display of your poor and constantly changing music choice.

I'm not a heartless hard arse. Letting go wasn't easy for me. I found the elimination process emotional. Just as I'm about to relegate an object to the 'garage sale' box, there is a sudden nostalgic pang and a memory comes flooding back. The children are small and sleepy-eyed, they are in their pyjamas shuffling into the bedroom with the hand-made Mother's Day card and a large badly wrapped gift. I'm sitting up against the pillows sipping my lukewarm tea lovingly made by my eldest daughter as part of the morning ordeal. I am suddenly optimistic. Perhaps the kids have actually got me something good. But no, it's a giant pig money box. The joke is that is says, 'Swear Jar'. The kids say I swear too much. This is their idea of a joke. I'm slightly insulted. Frankly I was hoping for slippers. I declare, 'It's amazing.' Then I start to panic. Where do I put it? It's grotesque. You never see pictures from *Home Living* where spaces are cluttered a giant pink money box with the words 'Swear Jar' emblazoned on the side. So I put it on my bedside table and hope it falls off. It lived there for months. Then piggy made his way to the top of a wardrobe where he has spent the good part of the last decade. Now piggy is outside on the lawn in the company of all the other items of my life that I have decided must go.

Perhaps some taste-challenged stranger will take him home and give the piggy money box to his foul-mouthed mother. When someone does I start to cry. Not a lot. Just a lone tear rolls down my cheek. My husband pats my arm: 'Feeling sentimental, darling?' I glare and snap out a generous, 'Fuck off.' Then I put a dollar in the swear jar which means I've made nothing on it because I only sold it for a dollar.

I'm self-conscious at my own garage sale. People come in and shuffle around, looking through your stuff. I can almost hear them thinking, 'Wow, I thought Mandy Nolan would have better stuff than this. It's a bit disappointing.' It's what I am thinking when I look at my stuff. I thought by my age I'd have better trash than this.

At a previous garage sale, a bloke came in and told me his daughter said, 'Is that really Mandy Nolan's house? I thought she'd live in a rich house.' I'm a stand-up comedian not a coke dealer!

The weird thing about a garage sale is that you just make up a price based on what you think someone might pay. People ask me questions like, 'How much for this ceramic angel?' I don't know. I hate it. I almost give it away then the capitalist opportunist takes over. I say $10. And they look unconvinced and say, 'I'll give you $5.' I think to myself, wow, you really want it. I would have given it to you. But now I'm locked in a garage sale power struggle. So I say, no, I wouldn't take less than $10. Then they leave and I'm left with the stupid angel that I end up taking to Vinnies. Two days later I walk past Vinnies and it's for sale for $20. I never knew it was worth that much. I consider buying it back.

My favourite phrase at a garage sale is '$2'. Because really, I think that's all anything should cost. Basically you are paying me for the privilege of taking my rubbish away. It's one less thing my husband has to pack in the trailer for the tip. It's such a racket. Clearly you don't want the stuff, but as soon as someone shows some interest, suddenly you're thinking, maybe this isn't such a piece of shit after all. Maybe I like it. Maybe I shouldn't sell it. What if it's actually good and I've sold it for $2?

One thing I've discovered at garage sales is that no-one wants stuff that's free. People don't trust free. There must be a catch. I've found it's easier to sell things for two bucks than it is to give them away. Every garage sale I have a box of CDs that I give away for free. I put out a box that says 'FREE MUSIC'. People are suspicious. Some demand to pay me. Like $2 will make it sound better. Some people even ask if it is any good. I don't know. It's free. Does it matter if it's any good? If it's not your scene, give it to someone you don't like. One chap came and took the whole box. I thought, wow, a music lover. But turns out he was an entrepreneur. He went up the road and sold them at $5 a pop.

I made a major garage sale boo boo. In my enthusiasm to get rid of my possessions I ended up putting out a box that said 'Free bras'. The box contained a selection of bras I've worn throughout the last 15 years, ranging from sweet lacy 10Bs to mother-fucking scary 18DDs. Giant open-mouthed maternity bras with snappy clips to sensible beige sports bras to water-filled wonder bras to a couple of the girls' triangle-shaped trainers. Garage sales on a main road are a cash boon – we were raking it in – stuff was just walking out. It was almost dark when I did the post-garage sale clean up and I overlooked a few items. Like the free bras box that was sitting on the footpath. Later that night I was lying in bed when I heard a young and clearly drunk male voice yell out, 'Hey mate, check this out, fuckin' free bras!' Then there was laughing. Actually there was a lot of laughing. The next morning I awoke to find every one of my old bras on display up the length of the main road – one hung from the hitching tree, another was on a stop sign, the maternity was half hanging out of someone's letter box. It took me nearly an hour to retrieve my unwanted underwear. Although I didn't get the one from the hitching tree because the homeless bloke sleeping on the bench seat took it to keep his apples in.

We sold stuff, we gave stuff away, we threw stuff out. It seemed just as we'd got rid of one tonne of stuff another tonne would turn up. I became ruthless. Occasionally I had a little twinge of remorse that perhaps I went a little too hard on the 'letting go'. But I wouldn't tell John that. No way, because I had won. Apart from the children, there is now nothing in our life that harks back to our previous partners. All the items we own, the chairs we sit on, the bed we sleep on – everything belongs to this relationship. While there are certainly things I miss, and things

I'll never find again, I like it that way. I find it weird sleeping on a bed that John or I shared with an ex. I don't want dried up ex-partner sweat, semen or menstrual blood on my mattress. I don't want to live in someone else's sex shadow ... Maybe it's purile or petty, but it always felt creepy to me to be serving a meal to John on the dinner set I got when my ex husband Russ and I got married. It made me feel like a terrible heartless slut.

'How many men have eaten on this dinner set?' cryeth the knave.

'None good sir,' replied the maiden, 'but I fucketh a hundred men on that bed.'

Now I'd purged myself of the possessions of my past, I was ready to start all over again.

BEIGE SWEET BEIGE

Orange is the happiest colour.

Frank Sinatra 1915–98

*E*skimos are regaled for their understanding of the nuances of white. In fact, it has been stated that they have something like a thousand words for snow. As it turns out, it's a bit of an exaggeration. Eskimos actually only have fifty words for snow. Not quite as poetic, but I guess when you are surrounded by snow day in day out, you get to know your snow. The ancient Egyptians had fifty words for sand. I would imagine they'd be variations of, 'Fuck! Hot sand', 'More sand', 'Fuck this sand' and 'Is that sand in your pants or a scorpion?' I guess the exaggeration of the existence of such an extreme lexeme is because there's so much of it. Snow and sand that is.

On reading a *Home Beautiful* magazine at the doctor's surgery the other day I have come to the conclusion that stylists and interior decorators have developed a thousand words for beige. I had no idea that there were so many slight variations. I just thought beige was beige. But apparently not. There is, according to colour experts, a whole world of beige waiting patiently to be found. Beige, I think you will find, is a very patient colour. It's not like red or purple. Those colours scream and throw tantrums or touch you on the arse or flash their tits. No, beige is well behaved. Sedate.

To me, beige is middle of the road. It's the 'please don't notice me', shy conservative wallflower of the colour palette. It is a colour without a conscience. Beige has no problem locking children in detention. Or stopping boats. In fact, beige is quite happy for refugees to linger for years in 'Processing Centres' – places as beige as the people who sent them there.

Beige always hands in tax returns. It's not surprising because beige is very often an accountant. Beige sponsors a world vision child but secretly fears the aboriginal family who moved down the road might affect property values. Beige likes to use sentences like, 'I have lots of gay friends' when they say something disparaging or bigoted about gay people to permit their homophobia. Beige also claims to have 'an aboriginal friend' and 'an Asian friend' but no Muslim friends. Beige is polite. Beige is efficient. Beige is quietly powerful. Beige voted for Tony Abbott. Beige would have sex with Tony Abbott if it could, and create more Tones of Beige to make everything 'nice' and 'safe' and 'sensible'.

Beige is not threatening. However, Beige is quietly powerful. While you are at work Beige sneaks into your house and screws your wife. Or husband. Or dog. Beige is the colour of true evil. Because Beige is innocuous, middle of the road, inconspicuous.

When you find someone dead on the carpet no-one would ever suspect Beige did it.

Beige has the perfect alibi. 'I'm Beige.'

We must rid ourselves of the pale evil of beige in all it's inoffensive, mild-mannered incarnations. There's Gnu Tan, Fiji Sands, Beige Royale, and for the woman on an alcoholic eBay bender, there's Self Destruct. Oyster Linen has become very popular, as has the vegetarian favourite Chick Pea. There's Hog Bristle or the bacon lovers and Puddle for the incontinent. The equestrian types get Jodhpur and there's even Bird Seed for the twitchers. For those of us who like to wear our pants a little too tight and our yokes a little too long, there's Camel Train. Not to be confused with Camel Toe, an uncomfortable shade of magenta. The list of beige variations go on. Pale Parchment, Curd, Grand Piano, Magnolia. Call it what you like, as far as I can tell, it's still frickin' beige. It seems like the colour fairies at Taubmans and Dulux have not just created 1000 words for Beige, they've also come up with 1000 words for boring.

The names are almost as bland as the colour. I would suggest something more invigorating, a colour name that is both challenging and self-aware. What about Fence Sitting Beige for the people pleasers? Or Boat Stoppin' Beige for the xenophobic what-if-it's-a-boat-full-of-terrorists-and-rapists-right wing, and yes-I-go-to-church-but-I-don't-pay-attention-to-the-bits-on-compassion types? There's Born to be Beige for people who used to live on the edge but had to move inland because the edge became terrifying when they kept falling off so they decided to play it safe.

Beige is also the colour of first world obesity, the giant beige fat roll that threatens to envelope and suffocate the globe.

Beige is ordinary. Unchallenging. When Beige sees injustice, Beige looks the other way. Beige justifies self interest. Beige lives in a nice house. On a nice street. Beige has a nice wife or a nice husband, and nice children. Beige drives a beige car. Beige doesn't have sex before marriage. Beige orgasms, but they are Beige too and only about once a year. Of course Beige goes to church. Beige lives a quiet life of Beige Desperation. And then when Beige dies, Beige has a Beige death. Nothing dramatic. Beige would never be eaten by a shark or overdose on heroin or be found choked to death in a decadent wanking mishap. No, Beige will just slip away. Then Beige will have a Beige funeral and people will gather and try and say something extraordinary about Beige but they can't. Because there's nothing extraordinary to say except the fact that they were Beige. Beige will be gone and no-one will remember. Which doesn't really matter because there's plenty more Beige where they came from.

As you can probably tell, I don't do Beige. At six foot tall and 90 kilos, with a big mouth and an even bigger attitude, I never really got the opportunity to be beige.

I am the kind of woman who comes in full colour. Sometimes bright and sparkly, sometimes dark and disturbed.

So when it came to choosing colours for the new house I had a pretty clear idea of what I didn't want. Knowing what you don't want, as far as I can tell, is the first step towards knowing what you do want. Generally if you eliminate everything you don't want you should be left with something you want. Usually. Unless you are such a difficult bitch you end up not wanting anything.

In the kitchen I rejected the plain look and went for white laminex with grey stripes. Behind the oven we opted for a bright citrus-green splashback. It is impossible to be depressed in our kitchen, it's that frickin' cheery. Even Sylvia Plath would have had a hard time gassing herself in there. (And of course the oven is convection.) We went for a dark grey feature wall with a stencilled moose head. Bright yellow cushions litter the couch. I painted my own technicolour indigenous-style art for the wall because I love it and that's as close as I'll ever come to an Elizabeth Kunoth Kngwarreye.

I love colour. Whether it's through paintings or cushions or wallpaper or furnishings, colour gives the spirit a lift. My soul sings when my eyes rest on the soft hues of a pale pink blanket, and I feel safe and sweet and happy. Ultramarine is the colour that takes me to a deeper place. It was Brett Whiteley's colour of choice, so now I call it Brett Whitely Blue, an opiated journey into Sydney Harbour. And yellow, bright canary yellow, splits me in two. If I immerse myself in the intense sunshine of it I get a glimpse of the place where Van Gogh found solace. The insanely terrifying sunniness of yellow.

I keep an art studio downstairs so I can immerse myself in colour. It's incredibly powerful. In fact it was the power of colour that got me painting in the first place. I guess I have to admit that I was stoned at the time, but now, even twenty years on, colour still has the power to draw me in and I don't smoke pot anymore. I realised early on that you didn't need drugs to find that altered state, although they certainly do help to short-track it.

Colour takes me to this wordless place, this intensely emotive intuitive zone. It's definitely my therapy. When you use colour you actually walk into your emotional state and float around like a dream. There's no need to rationalise, or to intellectualise, or even judge. Just be in it. For a dirty old cynic like me, this was such an intensely spiritual experience I kept it from my New Age friends just in case they thought I'd joined their ranks. I hadn't – I was still a nasty cynical bitch – I just experienced heightened states of awareness at two in the morning using the colour red.

Painting colour for me was this amazing emotional immersion. You have to be brave enough to let yourself sink to the bottom of it, because eventually you come bobbing up to the top with no idea of how long you've been there, or even what you have been painting. I would often pick one colour, like blue and I'd only use blue. I'd find deep hues, soft pastel almost transparent variations, then the dark impenetrable blocks of colour, brightness, deepness, darkness, softness.

When I was at my most vulnerable I spent hours falling into colour. I painted my way through broken relationships, heartache, self doubt, depression, fear and anxiety, into this place of hope. Colour gave me hope. I painted canvas after canvas, and what do you know, my therapy became my income. As fast as I painted them, I sold them. It was like the painting had become an archive of my mad journey back to me. I always found that rather amusing, that people would pay hundreds and sometimes even thousands of dollars, for the painting that was witness to the slow repair of my broken self.

I would have painted well over five hundred pieces over a ten-year period. I only have about two left. The rest found their way to other peoples' walls in their personal rage against Beige.

Somehow my personal paint-yourself-well-through-colour campaign worked. I still paint, but I seem to need to do it far less than I used to. In fact, it worked so well that when I sat down with the colour consultant (yes there is such a thing) and she bought out the charts detailing the endless range of colour choice at my fingertips, it was overwhelming. So much choice. In the end I chose beige.

Whisper White actually.

I guess being ordinary isn't that bad after all.

HOMEWORK

It always amazes me how hard people worked fifty years ago in comparison to how we live now. Imagine our stories when we're old — 'You don't know how good you've got it! I used to have to work two days a week ... from home!'

Ellen Briggs, comedian

After almost twenty years of working from home and wondering why I couldn't switch off, it finally occurred to me exactly why: you can't go home from work when you work at home.

Working from home has some definite positives, like reduced petrol consumption, zero office politics, no performance reviews by HR, no workplace bullying and the flexibility of being able to choose your own hours. If I want to send an email or file a document in my undies at 3 am then it's up to me. It just pays to be aware that emails will record the time they are sent, and some people may think you're nuts sending emails at that time.

I love working from home. There is no greater end-of-the-day thrill than not only fulfilling your work schedule but managing to squeeze in four loads of washing. Try doing your laundry in most average workplaces and someone is bound to file some sort of complaint about your 'breach of duties'. 'What, you have ciggie breaks – why can't I just pop on a load?'

On the downside, working from home means that work never stops. There is always a mountain of tasks building on your desk, threatening a paper-based avalanche. If you work at Woollies, you do your shift and go home. You don't curl up in the deli and sleep there. You go home and you don't think about work until you turn up the next day. Home life and work life are clearly delineated.

Not so for people who work from home. It's hard sometimes for me to tell where my home life begins and my work life finishes, they kind of bleed into each other. I have been halfway through an important phone conversation, about to close the deal when I've had the urgent 4-year-old call to arms: 'Muuuuuum!!! Wipe my bottom.' I have negotiated myself a handsome fee for service and wiped poo off a bum at the same time. My only regret is that I flushed. That whooshing sound of water really travels down a phone receiver. It occurs to me that the person on the other end of the line is going to think I am flushing because I was doing my business while doing business. How do you tell a person that you just wiped a child's bum? Instead I fudge with a, 'Wow, the surf is wild today, I'll just close the sliding door.' I am relieved that we haven't moved onto video calls because for people who work from home, our 'professional' cover will be blown to bits.

For a start, I'd have to get dressed. And give up 'Nude Tuesdays'. The chap who delivers my eBay parcels would be devastated. There was a point in my work at home career where I really slacked off in my personal grooming. It seemed ludicrous to be getting dressed if you weren't leaving the house. Some days I wouldn't get out of my jammies until four in the afternoon. I'd have a shower and realise I should probably put them on again. My daywear looked like it had been purchased from the Kath and Kim Tracksuit Collection.

When I'm not on stage being fabulous and funny – which in reality is only two or three nights a week – I spend my work days staring at a screen. In a room. On my own. It's a bit isolating. Thankfully I do enjoy my own company and have some wonderfully robust conversations with little ole me, but there are days when a person who spends so much time in their own company starts to drift into depression. Or, at the very least, mild despondency.

So I decided to dress every day like I am going to work. It's part of maintaining my self-discipline and wards off social decay. When you think about it, working from home should mean you're looking better, not worse, than when you went to a workplace. You're dancing to the beat of your own drum now, you're no longer one of the corporate zombies. Now I dress to impress – myself.

I wash my hair, blow dry and straighten, pull on a floral dress, making sure I show a enough tit to keep the eBay bloke punctual, maybe some pearls or dangly earrings, some strappy sandals, a spray of French perfume, a bit of slap and I'm done. And red lipstick. I always wear lipstick. It's my siren call to the world. I do this after the hour I spend making lunches and overseeing my adolescents' daily attempts to make the school bus stop. I ferry tea and toast and signed permission slips to various bedrooms, and then spend the last ten minutes standing at the front door with the car keys in my hand shouting, 'You've got three minutes. Car is leaving. That's three minutes. Now it's probably two and a half, that's two and a half minutes. Teeth should be brushed by now ...'

Working from home can become a bit antisocial. One of the benefits of a workplace is that it offers a new setting for informal chitchat. Those incidental and often meaningless conversations are generally pretty important in keeping you sane. A person may be working from home, but that doesn't mean you need to lose contact with the outside world. Every morning, after I am dressed for 'work', I go to the coffee shop where I chat with other people who don't work from home, and in some cases don't work at all. Most mornings someone says, 'You look dressed up today Mandy, are you going somewhere?' I generally just say, 'Oh just a big day of work.' I try and avoid saying, 'No, just going home,' because then it would probably seem just a little bit sad. Like I had got dressed up solely for the purpose of having coffee. Which I had.

Although it *is* Mullumbimby. This might seem rude, but I think it has one of the most casual dress codes in the country. Some people don't even wear pants. I once wore my French Jersey black pyjamas in to pick up a takeaway and the waitress commented, 'Wow, you look corporate today.' Wow, I was in my jammies. You can see how easy it would be to let yourself go in a town that thinks wearing PJs is overdressing.

One of the problems with working from home are the unannounced poppers. These are the people who just 'pop' over for a cup of tea. Or because they were bored. Or had to fill in time before an appointment. When you work at home people know that you are there. You are captive. If someone pulls up, best hide under your desk.

Fortunately people don't pop over as much without phoning first. Poppers perplex me because ideally, I'd like to be able to accommodate them with a nice relaxing chat and a cuppa. Like I used to do when I didn't have children or shit to do. But now I'm on a tight schedule. Daycare pick up is in two hours. A cup of tea and a chat will cost me $50 in fees and $400 in lost wages. If you are home and a friend comes over it's a bit rude to tell them 'Fuck off, I'm busy.' And the sad thing is, I'd love nothing more than to spend an hour with them. It's just that the boss gets the shits when I slack off.

It's funny who pops over when you work from home. I once had a lady turn up at my front door offering me a foot massage. I didn't know her very well, and clearly she'd been in my street and passing by when she saw me in the window and thought, well now is the time to make that unusual but very kind gesture. You don't expect strangers to be rocking up at midday offering you foot massage. She didn't just blurt it out up front. She came to the door and said, 'Mandy, you do so much for the community – I'd like to do something for you. I've come to give you a foot massage.' I should have said, 'Thank you, that's nice but I'm terribly busy,' but instead I let her in. If you come to my door offering foot massages then all my stranger danger training goes right out the window. It was a bloody good foot massage.

One of the biggest challenges for me working from home is that I am not only the boss and the employee, I am also the cleaner. I have to clean the entire workplace. If I went to work somewhere else I could drive out and leave it behind. But because I am there, I can't sit at my desk until the beds are made, the kitchen is clean and the floor is swept. My husband thinks I'm nuts. A bomb could go off in the lounge room leaving bits of couch strewn around the house and it wouldn't bother him in the least. He'd step over it on the way to his computer.

I can't stop noticing disorder. In fact, it's all I notice. I can't start work until the house is sorted. I don't know whether it's a stalling technique or a legitimate block to work. Or some sort of cleaning tantrum I need to throw to cope with the building anxiety of trying to manage an unmanageable workload.

I don't ever seem to finish work. There's an endless stream of emails to answer, phone calls to return, articles to write, people to interview, forms to fill in, applications to submit, submissions to prepare, invoices to send, accounts that need paying. I would have never thought that such a self-indulgent pursuit – that of being funny for money – would involve hours and hours of arduous creation, promotion, communications and bookkeeping. Of course, I leave the bookkeeping to last.

When one is caught in the process of trying to earn money from home, one can't be wasting time filling in silly little forms for the tax department. I don't think the tax department have a clue what it's like working from home, because they work at the fucking tax department. Maybe if they did their job from home they'd be a lot nicer. When they ring to ask, 'Why haven't you paid your PAYG instalment?' and I say, 'Oh I'm sorry I missed the date, I got caught up doing the washing,' they'd be completely sympathetic, because they would be doing their washing too.

The Tax Department needs to spend a week with someone who works at home to see just what happens and how hard a self-employed person has to work to make a minimum wage. That way they might stop making those pesky calls that start with, 'Amanda, what was the reason for your non-compliance?'

Clearly the answer is, 'I decided in the scheme of things, you weren't important.' They don't like this answer. But it's the truth. So I proceed with, 'I didn't have the money because all my income is invoiced and I thought that feeding the family and paying the electricity bill was more urgent than paying my tax in advance.' The tax man mumbles to himself. I explain further. 'I can invoice for a period but if no-one pays within that period then the income in that period is absent until they do pay. Kind of like me not paying you.' Tax man is astounded. 'So there are periods of no income?' Yes dickhead, there are.

Then tax man says, 'Amanda, tell me what it is you do.' I can't believe this. The dude is on the phone giving me shit for being non-compliant, like I have the earn capacity of Gina Rhinehart or Clive Palmer. We're talking $6K here. Tops. Not six hundred thousand or six million. We're talking, six little Ks. And the dude doesn't even know what I do for a job. Maybe he should earn his Ks by reading his file.

So I say, 'I'm a comedian.' Then tax man laughs and says, 'Very funny Amanda, what do you really do?'

Great, now the tax man is giving me shit. The dude is a heckler. A heckler who could garnish my bank account if he felt like it.

'I really am a comedian.'

'Oh, we don't have a box for that. I will just put actor.'

If I'm getting listed as non-compliant, I at least want to be listed for my actual job. 'I am a comedian. Put comedian.'

'I'll put entertainer.' Christ, now I sound like some sort of fruit loop who stands in the mall with juggling balls. In the end I give up, and agree to pay the $6K by instalment.

This working from home racket is great if you are some sort of amazing business head. But I'm a creative. I hate numbers. When I do my tax return, it's not just a matter of claiming one pair of sunglasses, two work pants and submitting my group certificate. It's a bloody ordeal. Preparing for my accountant takes a good month out of my work schedule. For a start I have two shoeboxes absolutely brimming with receipts, a stack of invoices and bank statements. I spend hours hunched over unscrunching bits of papers and typing 3 April 2014, pencils $2.30. Each and every transaction must be separately entered. It's like a financial autopsy. I get to reflect on every item of expenditure for the financial year.

One of the things I *do* love about working from home is my increased efficiency. The busier my life gets, the more I have to do, the more I get done. People only waste time when they have too much of it. I don't have time to procrastinate. I could only procrastinate if it was on my list.

Working from home means you are your own boss, so you kind of have to treat yourself like both boss and employee. It's not all long lunches and blow jobs, believe me. In fact, it's usually lunch at the desk and the only exposure to sexual harassment is when the cat starts rubbing himself provocatively around my legs because I couldn't be bothered feeding him. Why would I? It's not on my list buddy! I write lists of what I expect myself to achieve each day. I budget my tasks across the week. It helps reduce the anxiety, and I have to say, for those anally retentive list makers like myself, there is no greater joy than grabbing a pen and scratching it through a task. Done. Done. Done.

Although my work list probably looks a lot different to most work-at-home blokes. 'Write media release, finish chapter on 'Working from home', reschedule photo shoot, interview Joan Armatrading at 12, make pathology appointment for Zoe, pay internet bill, send headshot to new client, get Marilyn Monroe costume for Sophia's Halloween party, book parent–teacher interviews, move money into bank account for tax payment, book dog groomer, check hotel availability for upcoming gig, cook apple crumble for soup kitchen.' That's what is on my list today. I doubt many work-from-home dads will be banging out an apple crumble so their kids can do a shift at soup kitchen that evening.

I have always relished the delicious silence after everyone has left the house. For a work-at-homer, this is the sound of a busy workplace. About a year ago my husband, a long-time university academic in health, decided the bureaucracy was impeding his ability to implement innovative programs and so set up his own company to work from home. Of course I encouraged him. I said things like, 'Do something meaningful with your life. Don't waste the last fifteen to twenty years of your work life marking time in an atmosphere where no-one appreciates your genius!'

It hadn't properly occurred to me that when he started working from home, it would be our home. For a start, we only had one home office. Of course there was a 'chair' for John at my long computer desk, he just never used it, so all my stuff, my pencils, papers, files, envelopes, CDs, and general desk crap littered the space where he was supposed to sit.

At first John's work at home plan wasn't a problem as he didn't do any work. Because he was used to travelling long distances to go to work, his discipline was tied up with actually physically being at a workplace. He was a hard worker for other people but his first six weeks at home saw him ambling around like a moth looking for a bulb. He'd read a book, do some gardening, make me another cup of tea, call his mum and then ask me if I'd like to go out for lunch.

Setting your own agenda takes time. When embarking on a brand new project there is such an enormous scope of possibilities that it's basically atrophying. New work-from-home bloke looked a bit stunned. He had so much he could do that he now couldn't do anything. I knew what that felt like. It's the beginning of 'working at home' when there isn't actually any work yet. For new work-from-homers, the challenge is the twelve-month build. If work were a car, you'd have to not only construct it at home, you'd have to find all the fiddly little bits, work out how to put it together yourself, and maybe a year into it, you could go for a little drive. If you want to work at home, you have to be prepared for the set-up period where you establish what you do, how you do it, and why anyone else in the world wants what you do. It's a bit overwhelming when you could just make yourself a sandwich and a cup of tea and watch a bit of *Dr Phil.*

There is one workplace rule for we homers. No TV. Never TV. Not even TV at lunch. You have to remember that you are only one 'on' button away from being a depressed housewife watching *Oprah*, or *Judge Judy* or *The Bold and the Beautiful*, as opposed to a dynamic work-from-home mum.

John eventually made his way to the desk. I should have been thrilled for him. After all, I had encouraged him to take the jump into self-actualisation in his own business. But now my darling genius was only a metre away, in MY office. Well I guess it was technically OUR office. If one of us had to make a phone call, the other one had to leave the room. When he had a good idea, he'd get all chatty. I don't talk when I'm working. I just power away and look annoyed. Ask the cat. He'll tell you.

While I love my husband very much and desire no other, I found his presence irritating. I sleep with the dude, do I really have to sit that close to him at work? It was so intimate, I felt less like I was working and more like I was driving a taxi. One time I even leant across and asked John, 'Where would you like to go?'

He just looked puzzled. I'm used to that look so I did a U-turn and asked him to get out. I couldn't concentrate on my work with the sound of him tapping away. Or muttering to himself. Or scratching his balls. I was about to have the 'I think you need another office,' conversation when John announced, 'I think I need another office.' I was so hurt. I couldn't understand why he didn't want to work right next to me.

Once I got over being trumped on delivering the workplace rejection I began helping John convert our downstairs garage into his office. While our shared office is a 2.5 metre x 4 metre hole in the wall upstairs, John has a giant 6 metre x 6 metre luxury pad, with his own shower, bathroom and separate access if he chooses. We laid down flooring, painted the walls, installed a couch and a coffee table. I bought him a stereo for his record collection and whacko, John had a groovy man office. I haven't seen him since.

I was secretly jealous. His office was bigger and funkier than mine. And he seemed to be getting a lot done. He went in and closed the door and didn't come out until 5 pm every day. I stood outside the door and thought, 'Maybe he's just in there wanking.' I threw the door open and there he was staring intently at his computer on a phone headset talking up business. In his big impressive office.

Next year we're extending a deck out there, with giant glass bifolds and a walkway to the pool. Now I may work from home, but that doesn't mean I can't resort to some good old-fashioned office politicking. I pumped out a new business plan, and by the end of next year, if my plan to weedle away and undermine comes off, that office will be mine!

In the meantime, I'm just going to pop on another load of washing, make a cup of tea, and watch the teensiest bit of *Dr Phil.*

After all, I deserve it. And I'm a comedian, so it's not slacking off, it's research. I can even claim it on tax!

IN THE COMFORT ZONE

Surely everyone is aware of the divine pleasures which attend a wintry fireside: candles at four o'clock, warm hearthrugs, tea, a fair tea-maker, shutters closed, curtains flowing in ample draperies to the floor, whilst the wind and the rain are raging audibly without.

Thomas de Quincey, *Confessions of an Opium Eater*

I am in love with my new mattress. I mean it. I have never in my life gone to bed every night and felt such continuous satisfaction. My mattress is selfless. It is there to serve me. To hold me. To make me feel … alone.

I go to bed and I don't even know my husband is in there. He could be sleeping in the next room. Or even the next suburb. Hell, he could be having an affair, slipping out of bed once I've drifted off and sneaking back in the early mornings and I'd never know. Mr King is the space maker, the keeper of secrets. In fact, I'd even go as far as to say that in keeping us apart, my mattress is keeping us together. Gone are the days of the squeaky spring base hosting the foam valley that forced cohabiting couples into a sweaty embrace, whether they wanted to or not.

These days, if finance permits, one can have acres and acres of bed. The bed is no longer just a piece of furniture. The modern bed is part of the relationship. Why, it even offers 'support'. My mattress has coiled springs, it's ultra plush with a glorious cloud-like pillow top and, unlike me, it has a memory! My bed actually remembers how I sleep. And to think people in the past slept on sacks of wheat or rocks or bundles of palm fronds wedged in a corner. The average first worlder starts bruising at the thought. The disappearance of the hard bed is making us soft. These days I'm such a whinging twat I can't stay in a hotel if the bed is uncomfortable. I have been known to complain so much that my husband has cut the holiday short just so I'd shut up about the agony in my lower back. (Apparently if a man has to massage a woman's sacrum for 17 hours a day it's not a 'holiday'.) Somehow, and I'm not quite sure exactly how, pre-pillow top generations managed to survive and sleep in such low levels of comfort!

We have become obsessed with comfort. You may think I am stating the obvious, and in doing so there's an immediate assumption that if one's life is made more comfortable, rather than less, then we are moving in the right direction. Isn't that progress? Isn't it what we want? Let's face it, who doesn't want to be comfortable? Who doesn't want to live in what the Oxford Dictionary defines as 'a state of ease and freedom from physical constraint'? Unless you're some sort of spiritual ascetic hell-bent on finding god through suffering (there's some three-star hotels I could recommend), then your in tolerance levels will have been lowered by this constant exposure to the loveliness of comfort.

It's my theory, and possibly an unpopular one, that our pursuit of comfort has come at a significant cost to the planet and to ourselves. You see, the more tolerant of comfort we become, the less tolerant of discomfort we become. Yes, we've become a bunch of soft cocks. To create our comfort we've had to create a lot of discomfort for folks later down the line: nasty quality of life destroying discomfort like global warming and rising sea levels. It's hard to believe that evolving to the point of being able to cool down with the touch of a button on the air con would have us looking at a fast-tracked entropic future. As Newton suggested in his third Law of Motion, for every action, there is an equal and opposite reaction.

Does this seem a bit overly simplistic? Well, think about it like this. Use air conditioning to create the perfect 22–25 degrees and by the act of cooling, we have, in fact, created heating since our cool home comes at the cost of heating our world. Which, of course, then means we need more air conditioning, which means the planet gets hotter, and the air con just gets turned up a notch. It's the perfect capitalist formula, where consumption creates a market for increased and continuous consumption. There can be no product saturation. Just eventual planetary demise when the cranking of the dial crashes into our environmental denial. I guess there's only so long you can sustain a planet using the 'Dubai air con oasis in the desert' model.

Personally I don't like air conditioning. Especially not in the house. It's creepy. To me, sleeping with the air con on makes me think I've nodded off in the deli at Woolies. When it's hot, I like to sweat. When it's cold, I like to snuggle. It might be old-fashioned, but I don't think there's any great harm in experiencing extremes of temperature. Generally if it's hot, you can open a window, have a cold shower, frolic nude over the sprinkler or get so drunk you evolve beyond the need to have a 'fixed' climate setting. Conversely, if you are cold you can put on more clothes or wrap yourself in a blanket (one of those polyester snuggly ones do the trick) especially if you light a fire then collapse snuggly first into the open flames leaving the blanket to sear into your skin.

The evolution of air conditioning is interesting, as it shows the close parallel of the evolution of a product in direct alignment with the evolution of a belief about human comfort. Air conditioning was originally invented as a way to cool air for industrial purposes. Then, of course, what happened next is what always happens when someone invents a successful industrial product. The manufacturers went looking for other markets. Namely us. Wow, so that explains why living in an air-conditioned room feels like sleeping in a factory.

Air conditioning was the perfect solution for badly built high rise buildings. These structures were initially very difficult to keep cool with natural ventilation or to warm through thermal mass or insulation. If people were going to be packed on top of each other in high-density living, then they were going to need air con. It's not like you can run nude under the sprinkler 20 floors up.

Then some air-conditioning boffin hit on the idea that there is a science to human comfort. I don't think this had ever occurred to people before, as discomfort was just part of the human condition. In fact, discomfort was a way of life. In fact, people wrote songs and poetry about discomfort. Suffering was good for the creative process. People didn't need alarm clocks when their beds were as hard as a slab of wood. They got up because the pain of sleeping in was greater than the pain of getting up. The air-con scientists established that humans are most comfortable between 22 and 25 degrees and it would be true to say that, like vegetables in a crisper, we have become scientifically acclimatised to accept that comfort exists only in this 3 degree realm.

Soon the air conditioning concept crept into the residential realm, morphing architecture in its wake. Eaves were trimmed back or lost entirely as we built houses designed to be cooled or heated through air con alone. Until recently the cost of AC was about 20–30 per cent of the capital cost of a high rise and about 70 per cent of the running cost. Clearly this was never going to be a sustainable model. High-rise apartments have always reminded me of refrigerators stacked neatly full of nicely cooled human meat.

Global warming meant that this kind of building code had to be revised. Now we have building rules that insist we make our dwellings more energy efficient so we use less air conditioning to achieve the desired 22–25 degree range. We now include more insulation, thermal mass and natural ventilation to ensure that under most climate conditions, we can maintain our most human-friendly climate. While I appreciate the trend of moving away from air con, I still have concerns about this idealised temperature norm. What if some of us actually like getting a bit hot under the collar? It's also hard to give someone the cold shoulder if they're being artificially warmed.

And what if, as a new study is showing us, this constant need to control climate, to protect ourselves from climate extremes, is in fact one of the contributing factors in what makes us fat?

According to a new study, published in the journal *Cell Metabolism* (yes, one of my personal faves) it appears that 15 minutes in the cold may well be the metabolic equivalent to an hour of exercise. That's right, an hour in the climate-controlled gym jogging yourself into a lather of sweat on the treadmill is equivalent to 15 minutes in the carpark shivering your butt off as you rummage for your keys!

You see, fat isn't just fat. Our adipose tissue is divided into two types of fat, white fat and brown fat. White fat is that blobby stuff that bulges on our arses, guts and thighs. It stores energy, but generally later leads to us having chronic illnesses like heart disease and diabetes. Brown fat, which gets its colour from high iron content, generates heat and burns calories when stimulated. It is prevalent in infants but less abundant in adults. Brown fat is the good fat. White fat is the villian.

And guess what? Brown fat is created when we are cold. In the study the US National Institute of Health monitored ten healthy subjects exercising in a lab kept at 18 degrees celcius. Later the same subjects lay on a bed and the temperature fell to a shiver-inducing 12 degrees. The subjects all produced brown fat from their white fat, thus increasing their brown fat content and reducing their white fat. Until recently it was thought that we lose brown fat in infancy. As it turns out, we've just been heating ourselves fat.

And as every overweight girl who's lined up for a spray tan at the onset of summer knows, brown fat looks better than white fat.

So is there a connection between the increase in global temperatures and the obesity epidemic? Imagine the revolution of the diet industry if the message got out to 'Go to the fridge and lose weight.' That's right, 15 minutes a day standing with the fridge door open and you'll be shedding the kilos! That is providing of course that the temperature is outside of the established comfort zone. This leads me to another observation – perhaps we need to become used to being well outside our comfort zones. Comfort is making us sick. And fat.

Constant exposure to and the expectation of comfort is lowering our resistance to hardship and adversity. It has certainly reduced our resilience.

In my childhood there were endless opportunities of extreme discomfort to build my resilience. The car was the perfect example. In fact, I am considering ripping out the air-con unit in the car just so my kids get to experience some old-school driving heat.

You haven't lived until you've been squashed into an HR Holden with four kids on a bench seat sitting two up, two back, sweat gluing your arse to the vinyl, with only two hand straps for safety. The windows would be wound fully down with the wind burning your eyes and only a crackling country station for musical amusement. There was no surround sound, no velvety reclining seats, no safety belts, no temperature control, no iPods. No GPS. Just your mum in the front trying to read a map upside down with your dad swearing at her. And to top it off your mum and dad smoked all the way and invariably one of you copped a third-degree burn on your thigh from a discarded butt that was sucked back through the rear window.

And no-one stopped when you screamed. They just told you to shut up and stop being such a sook. When you arrived at your grandmother's there was no pool. No landscaped leisure area. No extra television. Television was in the lounge room and it was black and white and you weren't allowed to touch it because TV was only put on for the news and *A Current Affair* and maybe *Sale of the Century* if you were lucky.

And when you went to bed it was so hard that if you jumped on it you'd break your arse. This was the bed your father had slept on when he was a boy. The mattress was 40 years old. In fact, the combined age of all the mattresses in the house was over 300 years. People didn't replace things unless they were broken or burnt to the ground. They certainly didn't aspire to higher and higher levels of comfort.

Lounges were not giant leather modular leisure pits that they are now, designed to caress and enfold the sitter. Lounges were small and hard and very, very fucking uncomfortable. They were designed for upright sitting, certainly not reclining. For that matter, all chairs were hard and kind of brutalising. Chairs were designed and produced in line with the philosophy that you needed to get off your fat arse. No-one was supposed to be sitting for any length of time. Sit to eat dinner. Sit to watch the news. Chairs were not designed to watch the entire season three of *Game of Thrones* in one sitting. Life was about getting up, working hard, and then collapsing at night into your uncomfortable bed. Look what's happened with all these creature comforts encouraging us to lounge and sit and flap about like giant floppy seals. We've got lazy and diabetic and fat. It's ironic. Because being fat is about as uncomfortable as it gets.

So maybe if we want to lengthen our lives, to be less fat, to be less depressed and much happier, we need to start experiencing a little discomfort now and then.

Maybe it's time to ditch the air con.

I think it's called air con for a very good reason. It's a con.

Of course, I have no intention of surrendering my mattress. As a compromise I sleep naked with the window open. In winter. I've lost 10 kilos in ten nights.

Hypothermia is the new Weight Watchers.

I'll be getting into those slutty white Liz Hurley jeans any day now.

Brown fat, here I come.

THE HAUNTED HOUSE

*I can't tell you how irritating it is to be an atheist
in a haunted house.*

Matthew Tobin Anderson, writer

*T*here is a long tradition of storytelling around the theme of 'haunted house'. In fact, in most of the great spine-chilling films about spiritual possession and evil the eeriest character is usually the house.

I think all scary stories about ghosts and heads spinning around are about the dark forces that lurk when the lights go out. I have always loved watching scary movies. The thought that I could go to bed and wake up with my head doing a 360 gives me a peculiar thrill. It's been rather disappointing, but for all the different houses I have lived in, I haven't encountered a good old-fashioned haunting. I've often wondered, 'What's wrong with me?'

The closest I got to any paranormal activity going on in my house at night was the cat pulling down a possum. If you've ever heard the shrieks and screams of what actually lives in your roof, then you could mistakenly think you were part of a casting call for *Amityville Horror*. Yes the house is a burial ground, but not for native American Indians, or previous human occupants: most of the dead tend to be rats, snakes, possums and family pets.

When you think about it the home is the obvious setting for horror, the perfect location for suspense. The family home is ordinary, our safe haven from the world. It's the place where we let our guard down, have a shower, sleep, walk around in the nude. Home is where we relax. Relaxing makes us vulnerable. Enter the poltergeist. If a poltergeist had a go at you in a restaurant or a hotel then you'd leave. It's hard to complete a good haunting story when the victim leaves. The victim needs to stay. The victim needs to be at home. That way the spooky visitors get to play out a decent plot line. I watched the *Amityville* series while screaming the whole time at the TV, 'Get out! Leave now! It's in the house! Are you fucking idiots?' I don't think the movie would have been as enjoyable if they spent the last forty minutes making tea and watching telly in a hotel room down the road.

I don't know how they don't know. To me 'abandoned farm house' screams DEMON. From the moment a family drives to the rusted iron gates on the abandoned country manor, always bought for a song, I'm nervous. Clearly there's been a murder suicide. Someone must have hung themselves in the attic. There's an ancient burial ground in the basement. The place is pure evil. Get the fuck out!

Oh god, don't let the kids sleep there by themselves. Turn around. Turn around now. But no, they take the labrador, the kids and the station wagon up the drive, optimistic that this is going to be the setting for their amazing new life. The house is always huge. A formerly grand residence now in virtual ruin. I think if you are moving into a formerly grand residence you should not only get it fumigated for pests, you should get an exorcist in.

Dad will get his hammer out and start nailing down the boards on the verandah while Mum fusses in the kitchen. Tinkly piano music plays. The kids explore the attic and of course they generally find an old photograph hidden in the wall or a broken doll with an eye missing, and before long the kids are entered into some sort of contract with the devil. It's very hard to embark on a new life when your family is possessed by demons. Happy families fall apart in haunted homes. You know at the very least the dog isn't going to make it. The dog is always the first to go.

Ever since the tender age of four when my eldest daughter chirped, 'Mum we're all toys and God has been playing a game with us forever,' Zoe has been obsessed with the idea that someone must have died in our house. Every single one of them. I tried to explain that people die in houses all the time, it doesn't make them haunted. People have to die somewhere!

In our last house she was convinced that someone must have hung themselves in her room and that there was a murder in the living room by the fireplace. I was curious as to why she would be saying that … maybe the neighbour's kids had mentioned something in passing. I've seen the films, I know that no-one tells you upfront you are living in the killing zone, it's something that leaks out slowly. She said, 'Oh, no-one said anything. I just made it up. It feels like someone could have been murdered there. If you were going to kill someone you'd do it there for dramatic effect.' Wow, I'd never thought psychopaths were sensitive to Feng Shui too. 'Excuse me, person whom I am about to dismember, I was wondering if you'd mind escorting me to the living room, it's so much moodier in there!'

Houses don't have to be haunted to have a spooky feeling. They have been the silent witness to the stories of people past. Families, couples, singles who have fallen in love, had babies, laughed, cried, got angry, sad, betrayed someone, drank too much, punched a hole in the wall, punched a wife, molested a child, threatened to kill, committed suicide, and then moved out. You just don't know what story a house carries with it when you move in. Where the unseen shadows fall.

To me that is a kind of haunting, a kind of human stain left by the footprint of human habitation. Our happiness, our sadness, our joys and our griefs, our best and most hideous selves, all housed somewhere behind the walls of home. It made building a new house reassuring, especially for Zoe. This was the first time she believed she wasn't living in some sort of historic crime scene. Any haunting was going to happen by us. We were the first offending family to make our mark, to leave our ethereal life stain in those hard to reach places.

Houses are the creepiest I think when they are empty. Standing in the empty rooms of a house where you once lived is perhaps the strangest of all, because you are standing in room full of your own ghosts.

Having been a long-term renter I have seen a lot of places, and thought, 'I wonder what has happened here.' Nice things and horrible things happen everyday to everyone. I guess something horrible has happened in most houses at some point and something horrible happening to someone else doesn't necessarily mean that something horrible is going to happen to you. Still, given the choice, if I knew that someone had killed their family in my bedroom, regardless of how long ago it was, I wouldn't want to sleep in there. I wouldn't buy a house with a dark history.

I think real estate agents would do well to take note. People want to know that the place where they hang their hat was lucky for someone. We all want to live in lucky places. Places where good things happened. Regardless of whether or not we are superstitious or believe the 'energy' of a place actually exists, most people are attracted to positive energy. For example, which house would you view?

'Newly renovated 5 bedroom, 3 bathroom home, modern appliances, 2 decks, views, double lock-up garage, parents retreat, pool and outdoor entertaining area. Previous occupants had 3 happy, functional and now high-achieving children, a happy and strong marriage, both going on to live fully actualised lives. Both are slim, in good health, have no signs of early onset dementia and have just retired to a country house in the South of France where they grow lavender and olives.'

'Newly renovated 5 bedroom 3 bathroom home, modern appliances, 2 decks, views, double lock-up garage, parents retreat, pool and outdoor entertaining area. Previous occupants had 3 children, one ended up a meth addict and is now a prostitute, another is in prison for rape and the other got cancer and died before his 12th birthday. The marriage failed, with the husband having affairs and the woman becoming suicidal. The woman has been diagnosed with early onset dementia, the husband was found to be a paedophile and after serving time is now in a community placement program. The wife is selling up as she's going into nursing care.'

Tell me honestly, which house would you buy?

Many years ago I moved with my husband (number two) and my three kids from the city to a gorgeous rambling country house. We'd been living in a two-bedroom house in Sydney's inner west. While it was neatly appointed there was something harsh and unnatural about it. Everything was paved or tiled or concreted. The only grass my children got to touch was 50 metres down the road at the street's 'common' – a small grassed park for families like ours that were living in semi-detached housing with no yard. This would have been suitable if it also wasn't the place where everyone took their massive dogs to take a shit. On any given day there would be no less than fifty turds steaming in the blinking sun.

One day I complained to my husband Russ that I couldn't take it, I couldn't have my children's childhood happening here.

I didn't care, I was going back to the country. I think he was sick of it too because he didn't protest that much and when I told him I'd found us a three-bedroom country house with a sunroom, an office, wrap around verandahs and a deck looking out onto the rolling hills he was definitely interested. Mentioning that it sat on 8 acres, had a tennis court and an ancient rainforest remnant was the clincher. We were off.

In retrospect I should have been worried. After all, the husband and wife and the three kids leaving the city life behind, pulling into the driveway of the new 'isolated' shabby chic country house … isn't that the plot for the haunted films that I had previously shouted at, 'Get out! Turn around!' Somehow, when you are turning into the driveway to your new dream life, you choose to turn that recording off. Holy crap. We were even in a station wagon.

The house wasn't haunted per se. But it had a pretty strange story.

The house was the oldest in the district. It had been the first home in the area and belonged to the family who had been credited as being the first white settlers there. It was a farming area and hadn't been settled that long – the house was from 1910 or 1920 or thereabouts. The house certainly had that well-occupied feeling, the walls were rosewood and the floorboards a solid teak. It was clear a lot of feet had trod those floors, a lot of hands had hammered nails into the rosewood to hang family portraits. In Australia our old houses are barely over a century old, and I often wonder what it must be like to live in house that's three hundred years old. I wouldn't sleep. I'd be too aware of all the ghostly fingers trying to pull back the sheets.

This story was told to Russ by a member of the original family. He was a farmhand for a big macadamia property a few kilometres down the road. He used to come and visit my husband from time to time. He didn't talk to me, he was far too shy. He was probably in his early fifities, unmarried and not used to women. Winston was one of those country blokes who takes his hat off when he sees a lady, muttering 'G'day Mam, is your husband home?' with eyes downcast from the bottom step. That kind of old-fashioned charm was unusual: I was used to men leaving their hats on and looking right at my tits.

Generations of Winston's family had lived and farmed there for well over 50 years. Unfortunately they'd fallen on hard times and the bank took the property and the house. The land was divvied up into smaller parcels and the house was sold. Many years later the house was occupied by a police officer and his young wife and baby. One day when the police officer was at work the son of the original family returns with a shotgun and takes the woman and child hostage. There's a siege. No-one was hurt, but the son ended up in a mental health institution. Russ told me this in bed one night the day before he was heading down to Sydney for a week's work.

I was petrified. 'Fuck! What if he comes back?'

'He's not coming back Mandy,' Russ said very pragmatically. 'That would have happened in the 70s.'

I wasn't so easily convinced. 'I've seen *Cape Fear*. The guy gets out. He comes back.'

For the week Russ was away I kept checking under the station wagon, half expecting to find Robert de Niro clinging to my exhaust pipe. Of course no-one ever came to take me hostage. I don't know whether I was relieved or disappointed. It didn't matter, because once I heard that story I was a wreck. I'd lie in bed at night listening for intruders. It's amazing how many bush noises sound like a psychopath coming to kill you.

Possums rooting in the ceiling had me convinced the attack was coming from above. The bush turkeys nesting under the house had me considering that he'd dug a trench and taken up residence below. And if you've never heard a randy koala growl then you don't know real fear. How can something so cute and cuddly sound like a 140-kilo rapist? Suddenly my country retreat felt like a time bomb. I was convinced we were going to be taken hostage, if not by an ageing psycho then by one of the giant huntsmen spiders that watched us black and glassy eyed from our walls. And when I say giant, I mean bigger than a man's hand.

Now that was some scary shit. In a way I have been taken hostage, but it was by my fear rather than an actual predator. Night terror was instilled in me as a child. My mother was widowed at twenty-seven and left on her own with two small children. She had this constant fear of her home being broken into and being murdered in her sleep. Ironically, she was more at risk of harm in the home when my father was alive. After all Dad was a binge drinking, black-out alcoholic with the disposition of Jekyl and Hyde. He'd verbally and physically abuse my mother when drunk – then wake up in a state of deep shame and self repulsion. He was a loving man sober who became angry and violent when drunk. One time he broke her collar bone, another time I remember the legs of a chair crashing through the door of the room Mum had locked us in. He cried over cruelty to animals but kept a gun in the house which always kept Mum on the edge. Mum's anxiety about danger didn't die with my father, it haunted her for years after. It's no wonder because our family home was less like heaven and a lot more like hell.

Statistics show that you are at greatest risk in your own home. You'll probably die there. Bathrooms and kitchens can prove the most dangerous places, and as for people most likely to cause you harm, have a good look at your life partner. It's a cheery statistic to realise that if you are murdered it's most likely to be by the person who shares your bed. Children are more likely to be beaten or sexually assaulted in the home, be poisoned, and fatally injured either by a mauling by the family dog or Mum's erratic Range Rover reversing. Yes, the home is fucking dangerous. If you were really safety conscious I guess you wouldn't go home at all. If you want to live, stay on the footpath.

After my Dad died my mum insisted on sleeping with all the windows closed and the toilet light on. We lived in Western Queensland so there were a few 45 degree plus airless nights when I was tempted to open the windows to let the rapists in just so I might get a little breeze.

It was the leaving on of the toilet light I found the most peculiar. It gave Mum a sense of security. If Mum had the toilet light on she could sleep in peace. She believed nothing bad would happen if she had that on. Who needs a man when you have an incandescent bulb? I don't know what message that sends to intruders. Maybe if they're light photophobic they might think: 'Oh bugger, I was going to break in but I can't, they've got the toilet light on.' To think all those stupid people install fancy security systems and all they needed was to leave the toilet light on.

This led me to believe that sex predators could be deterred by something as simple as a bit of lighting. When out at night I always recommend my girls carry a rape whistle and a torch. 'Kick em in the balls, blow your whistle then shine that light on the dirty fuckers.' That'll learn 'em.

I now believe that the toilet light had some magical powers of protection, because I have to say the entire time Mum switched it on, no-one burgled, raped or murdered us.

So now I am determined to make sure our family abode really is a sanctuary. On the home front I am the Health and Safety Officer. 'Don't run with scissors, don't leave water on the tiles, don't test if the kettle's on by putting your ear to it, get your head out of the oven, no forks in the toaster, no leaning over the balcony to wave goodbye to grandma ... and for god's sake, leave the toilet light on!'

THE JOY OF SOCKS

*He may be president, but he still comes home
and swipes my socks.*

Joseph P Kennedy

The home is the place of ordinary magic. It's important to remember that when you are being worn down by the mundane. There are stories that happen all around us that we are completely oblivious to. Take socks for instance. Innocuous foot coverings that reside in washing baskets, top drawers and, more often than not, discarded in tiny sock bundles on the floor. Ever since the first human invented socks by gathering animal skins around the ankles to soothe sensitive tootsies, socks have bamboozled us. Why do they never stay together? Where do they go? There is no doubt that socks are mysterious. I've lost hundreds of the little buggers. In fact I think if anyone ever sells socks in threes than we will have a sock-lution.

The other day a friend told me how she'd bought some expensive thigh-high socks on ebay and how devastated she was that one had gone missing in the first wash. I can understand that happening with the anklets or even a standard walking sock, but this designer sex kitten sock was over a metre long. How do you lose a sock that big? It's like losing a leg! Surely it would have to turn up somewhere.

I want to make a video called 'The Secret Life of Socks'. I need to know what happens. We need to stop accepting that they just disappear and start finding out where they actually go. Like CSI for socks. They must be somewhere. They can't just disappear entirely. I mean, maybe they're a higher life form – we've looked into space to find intelligent life, but maybe instead of looking up we should have just looked down and taken note of our socks.

I am not alone. It's not just my socks, it's my friends socks, my children's socks, my mother's socks. In every house in every street is a drawer full of lone socks. These are the socks that remain. The reliable sock. The sock that chose to stick by you. I appreciate the loyalty of the sock who stays and so I keep it. It's hard to throw a perfectly good sock out. I keep them in a draw like one day I'm going to find a use for single socks. They could become a new environmental friendly energy source: cars, lights, whole streets powered by remaining socks.

A lone sock is pointless. Last count, I have 54 lone socks. I know I should throw them out. But I keep them just in case. I suppose it's cruel to keep their hopes up. They lie in wait, like war widows waiting for a soldier who will never return. I'm thinking of setting up a RSVP-styled website for lone socks looking for their sockmate. Imagine the profiles: '16-year-old tartan walking sock seeks partner, preferably cotton blend with reinforced heel. Likes bushwalks, tennis and curling up in a ball.'

When M Sock Peck wrote *The Sock Less Travelled*, I believe he was talking about the sock who stays behind. The sock that likes to play it safe. The sock that stays is not a risk taker. It's a scaredy sock, hiding up the back of the sock drawer in its lonely unmatched shame.

Socks start out monogamous, entwined in a tight huddle with their identical life partner. To the outsider it's like a marriage of souls. The sock is illusive. Even the nosiest feet have no idea about what goes on in the mind of a sock.

One sock wants commitment, a mortgage, a regular job and kids; the other sock wants adventure. Wants to be reckless. Wants to make out with other socks. One sock wants to live on the edge, to discover its true self, to expand its horizons, to climb mountains, get a job on *Play School* as a sock puppet or enjoy the great outdoors holding a tomato plant to a trellis.

The other sock wants to watch TV and wear fluffy slippers. These socks may look the same, but deep down they want entirely different things. Neither of them are wrong. The adventure-seeking sock feels oppressed and starts to resent the boring sock. The stay-at-home sock. It loves its matching sock so it makes the compromise. It stays. But it comes with a cost. You can't just push down that kind of hunger and expect it to go.

Hunger turns inward and eats you from the inside out. And so the compromised sock gets depressed. Starts drinking. Withdraws. The sock starts to feel resentful. Starts downloading pictures of lone socks on the internet when matching sock is asleep in the drawer. Starts reading online blogs from socks living on the edge. This deeply conflicted sock fantasises about leaving. In fact, there's not a moment in the day when the thought of the possibility of a life outside the shoe does not taunt this poor sock.

This sock is in trouble. Serious trouble. How can safe sock, boring sock, the nice quiet compliant stay-at-home sock not even notice? How can the sock who stays be happy when matching sock is so sad? Matching sock must leave. Matching sock must go. Every shoe that comes off, every washing load, every trip to the dryer is an opportunity. The problem is, safe sock is always there. Watching. Then one day it happens.

The little sock with dreams gets stuck in the toe of a boot, or dropped by the car in the dark at a soccer oval, or wedged up the back of the laundry basket and makes a run for it. Curls in a ball and rolls. Rolls towards the endless possibility of a life beyond confinement, and duty and the dreary limitations of role. This searcher, this adventure sock finds the portal in the fabric of the universe. And guess what? This parallel universe inhabited by a master race of one-legged humans who struggle to solve a perplexing mystery … How is it they put one sock in the wash and come out with two ?

So I guess what I am really saying, in this allegorical tale of two socks is, which sock are you? The sock that stays or the sock that goes?

A ROOM OF HER OWN

My bedroom is my sanctuary.

Vera Wang

You can tell a lot about a person by their bedroom. Whenever I go to people's houses that I don't know very well, I can't help but have a little peek in their private chamber. They'll pop off to the loo, or to answer the phone, and I'll take a little wander hoping for at least a glimpse of their sacred space. It's like seeing a person in the nude. Not that I line up at windows waiting for someone to get their gear off, it's actually more interesting than that. The bedroom tells you what is underneath, it's the private space, the space not generally for show – unless of course they live in a caravan and the bed comes out when they collapse the kitchen table.

The bedroom is the place where a person sleeps, makes love, gets dressed, thinks, reads, talks, laughs and sometimes cries. I do most of my crying in my bedroom. Curled up like a child, the bedroom offers a place to sob, whether it's from real injustice or the hormonal harassment of a monthly menstrual cycle that can at times bring a girl to her knees. (And anyone else in her trajectory.) If you like to feel sorry for yourself, then there's no better place to do it than in the bedroom.

Bedrooms hold the emotional energy of a person's private self. This is the self we don't show to many people. The place where we don't wear make up, or brush our hair, or even suck our gut in. This is the place where we fart, pick our nose, check the dimensions of our pimply arse and bitch about our best friends. This is the place that houses the raw self – the one that exists before the clothes go on, social contrivances are adopted and the mask a person wears is strapped on to face the world.

We all do it. I don't think it means that we are dishonest people. I think it's impossible to show who you are all the time to all the people you know. If we did we'd be living in social isolation for fear of offending ten people before 10 am. I think its been pretty well established that lying is a necessary survival tool, and when used in the right circumstance, we don't even call it lying, we call it being 'tactful'. It often strikes me that the person who leaves the house is not always the same person who returns home.

I am curious when I look at someone's bedroom about how closely the picture of who I thought they were matches who they actually are. Of course, you shouldn't make too many generalisations from the angle of a doona cover, or the particular shade of pastel chosen for someone's drapes. You shouldn't ... but I always do. I make up whole personality profiles based on the weave of a woman's shag.

While I recommend having a sneaky sideways at someone's boudoir, I also suggest that you don't get sprung. If a person comes back from the toilet and finds you standing in their bedroom checking out their etchings, you better have a bloody good excuse.

'How embarrassing! I got lost,' doesn't cut it in a two-bedroom apartment. In fact I think it's even suss in a sprawling six-bedroom McMansion. If you *are* caught uninvited in someone's bedroom, here are a few excuses you might want to run with.

'Thank god you are here. A giant spider ran in here from the kitchen and I was worried it would jump on you in your sleep. Quick, go get a glass and a piece of paper.'

'It's so weird, I heard someone calling my name. I could have sworn it came from in here.'

'I work part-time for an interiors magazine and I just love what you've done with your bedside ashtrays.'

'I have always fancied you. I was going to ask you to fuck me. But I've stolen a pair of your undies instead. I'm wearing them now.'

'I'm looking for a location to shoot a film about a murder suicide and this place is frickin' perfect.'

'I had this dream that we found a suitcase of cash under your bed and I just had to have a look.'

'I am in here looking at your bedroom making some very personal and quite possibly unfair judgements about you.'

'I am sorry. I am a perve.'

Over the years I have used my bedroom to express my uniqueness. I have strung fairy lights around the window, then lay in the twinkling glow worrying that the Made in China lights are going to set fire to the house. I've used muslin to create an Arabian draping effect, I've painted walls, hung paintings, strung pearls, colour coordinated the hanging of my clothes and shoes.

If I entered my bedroom and looked around as if I didn't know whose bedroom it was, it would take me only a few moments to come to the conclusion that, 'This person is trying too hard to make a good impression. She's a control freak. She's insecure. But man does she have great taste in linen!'

I have also been very guilty of using far too many candles. I love candles. I don't know why. If I had my way I would buy a new candle every day. Lighting candles makes me happy. Don't get me wrong, I also like expensive lighting, I just prefer the boho charm of a hundred flickering flames.

You don't get candles without spending a lot of time in candle shops. My husband always looks like a hostage when I force him to accompany me into the den of my wax dealer. I can't believe he doesn't really want to have a good look around. To him, a candle is something you use when you are camping, or in a blackout, or maybe when you are trying to pull a root with a chick obsessed with candles.

He once stopped breathing for almost a minute when I let slip that one of the larger, more impressive candles residing in our ensuite was a bargain at only $69.99. A bloke generally can't get his head around why anyone would spend that much money on a light source that only lasts 20 or 30 hours max. 'But it smells amazing and it's so pretty,' I said weakly. He once even tried to tell me that candle expenditure was not in our weekly budget. I couldn't believe it. That's like removing fruit and veg. I like to think of it less as a light source and more as therapy. Candle therapy. Like somehow that on returning home and entering my boudoir that I will suddenly enter a deep stage of candle lighting relaxation – a state that a stress head like me can't reach with LED alone. While I enjoy the power of the dimmer, there's nothing quite like the warm leaping light of a hundred candles. And besides, electricity isn't fragrant. The candle is not just a light source, it's a sensual beast.

When you share a bedroom and an ensuite with a man, candles are a necessity. While I love having a bathroom and toilet for my own private use, I sometimes resent my husband leaving bits of beard in the sink and pubes on the soap. I also find the idea of someone taking a shit only metres away from the place where I lay my head a little unsettling. It's amazing how quickly a candle can restore olfactory equilibrium. My husband thinks taking a dump in the ensuite bathroom is fine. What he doesn't get is that it's fine for me, not for him. Because I only do it when he's out. Since he's started working from home, I've become a little uncomfortable.

The other thing my husband doesn't get is my love of cushions. And let me clarify something – a cushion is not a pillow. A cushion's sole purpose is aesthetic rather than utilitarian. The cushion is not about providing head or lower back support or being a place to balance your cup of tea. A cushion is about texture and colour. It's got nothing to do with function. Cushions are generally for display and should not be sat upon. You may occasionally use a cushion as a bolster, or as head support on the couch or while sitting up reading a book, but cushions, it must be understood, serve a higher purpose.

Cushions are a thing of beauty and should never be randomly tossed around willy nilly, like there was some sort of explosion in the Manchester department. Cushions are meant to be assembled. Arranged in size and colour to create pleasing combinations of softness and texture. I take cushion arranging seriously. I have so many of them. I have fluffy cushions, shiny cushions, hand-sewn cushions, novelty cushions, designer cushions, outdoor cushions, furry cushions, linen cushions, bland cushions, ornate cushions, silky cushions, felt cushions and spiky cushions. I think if most men had a choice they would have no cushions at all.

I don't think my husband John likes my cushions. In fact, I'd even go as far to say that he wishes them actual harm. I suspect when I am away that he throws them on the floor, chews the corners, or worse, that he uses them to sit on!

John goes out of his way to create chaos and disturbance in my highly controlled cushion assemblage. On our bed we have two pillows each. So that's four pillows. Pillows, as far as I am concerned, don't count as cushions. I have two European pillows. I don't know why they are called European and if Europeans actually use the 26 inch by 26 inch monstrosities. Maybe their necks are longer or their heads are bigger than ours. They're uncomfortable, but they look nice and are a fabulous foil for my cushion collection, so Europeans are always welcome on my bed.

Also on the bed I have two frilly green satin cushions, a grey-and-white hand stitched cushion, a charcoal felt shag cushion, two pale grey long cushions with charcoal felt flowers, one felt weave cushion, oh and then there's the black and white $150 cushion I got from Country Road, on sale for a bargain at $60, and the Taj Mahal black-and-white print cushion I got from Target. When it comes to procuring a good cushion, a girl has to cast her net wide. So, without counting my pillows, that's nine cushions, eleven if you count the Europeans, all perched neatly on my bed.

John and I sleep with one pillow each. Every evening the cushions must be neatly stacked against the wall so that one can gain access to the actual bed. Every morning when I remake the bed I carefully replace the cushions in the arrangement that I have deemed most pleasing. John knows this arrangement. But he won't replicate it. Ever. He assembles them randomly. He places them asymmetrically. Some backwards, upside down, tipped onto their little cushion fronts! He leaves some on the floor and the other day he had one in the toilet. I can't even let myself think too long about just what he might have been doing to it, but all I can say is that it hasn't sat straight since. If John makes the bed without my assistance, I know that I will have to return to fix the anarchy amongst my darling cushions. Honestly, talk about a problem. (Him, of course, not me. I'm normal.)

It has been suggested to me that I have a problem with cushions. In fact a close male friend hinted that I may have something akin to a cushion addiction. I don't even think there's a support program for that. Although I guess if I do hit rock bottom, at least I have something to cushion the fall! I don't think I have a cushion problem. I think it's a gender thing, kind of like being aesthetically challenged. I do think its heterosexual bloke specific, because my gay and lesbian friends seem au fait with flamboyant cushion displays.

So I did a cushion audit, to prove my husband and my judgemental meddling cushion-phobic friend wrong. Okay, so I have nine on my bed, alright I'll concede the Europeans so that makes eleven. I have seven cushions on my 13-year-old son Charlie's bed. John warned me that I need to back off as the overcushioning of a teenage boy's bedroom could be perceived as an attempt by the mother to emasculate and control. Bullshit. It's just more places to hide the tissues!

Charlie loves cushions. I know this because he shows the cushions respect. While he never gets it exactly right, his attempt at replacing the cushions on his bed is way above average for his age and gender. I am hoping he might be gay. Then I'll have someone to go cushion shopping with.

I have a friend who comes to stay who is so nervous about replacing the cushions in the assigned order he actually photographs them so he has an image to work to the next day. Gary, I should add, is always welcome to stay.

I have only four cushions on my five-year-old Ivy's bed. I have ten cushions on the upstairs lounge. There are seven on the downstairs lounge. There are another ten cushions on the balcony lounge. Four out the back. I have eight cushions on the fold-out and the leather swivel chairs in the rumpus. My 19-year-old Zoe has six cushions, and seeing as Rachel is away travelling in Europe, I've upped her cushion carriage to eleven. My 15-year-old Sophia has seven cushions. I also have twelve outdoor cushions for sitting on around our outdoor fire. It's cradle to grave for me with the cushions. The cushions come in the front door, go to the lounge, maybe a bedroom, and they move around the house enjoying various colour combinations before they become soiled or mouldy, or chewed, or have something weird happen to them in the bathroom, and then they go outside to use, and eventually when they are no longer fit for even that, they go on the fire pit straight to the big couch in the sky.

So to date, that's ninety-seven cushions. Alright, if it's an audit, I'll come clean. I have three new cushions hidden in the closet. So I have a hundred cushions. Woops, I neglected the day bed out the front and the outdoor setting. That's another ten cushions. That's a person to cushion ratio of 15:1. Sure it's high, but I think it's just the high side of normal. I'm still within a healthy cushion-owning percentile. I think if it was 20:1, I'd have to accept that at any point my family might decide to do one of those *Dr Phil*-style interventions. Anyway, I am thinking that it's not just décor, it's a hobby. My new line to anyone who dares to suggest I have too many cushions is, 'Oh, yes, I do have a lot, but then I am a collector.' Collectors have a lot more rope when it comes to indulging in their obsessive traits.

I think this whole bedroom-sharing thing that you do when you are coupled is a bit counter-intuitive. I mean, don't we fight our way to the top of the food chain to get a room to ourselves, the biggest room, the best room, and then we fuck it all up by sharing it with some bloke who thinks the idea of a little bit of decorating means installing a Rabbitohs flag above the bed.

I find the idea of the marital bedroom strangely perplexing. I love my husband, and he's well worth the sacrifice of surrendering half the room, and half the bed, but he's also using half the closet space. This seems ludicrous. I think one quarter would be more than adequate.

John's shirts hang in the spots where my frocks should be. Where his half of the wardrobe is sparse and roomy, mine is bulging at the seams. One more wafer-thin coat-hanger wedged onto the rack and the whole thing could just blow – my walk-in wardrobe has become a hair-triggered incendiary device of designer evening dresses, sparkly cardigans, beach smocks, peasant skirts and billowing blouses. I have shoes still stacked in their boxes. Shoes in baskets. Shoes in bags. I have to choose them by memory.

I often lie in bed looking at our shared wardrobe plotting a takeover. I mean, he's a man. He could live out of a suitcase. I, on the other hand, am a woman of a certain age with a certain penchant for shopping. And so I make my move, one frock at a time. In twelve months from now I will have claimed an entire rack.

In my mind I build my next bedroom. This is the room that has not just a walk-in closet, but a walk-in dressing room as big as my room. And it has floor to wall mirrors, special shoe shelves that offer rotating display, drawers for brooches, racks for earrings, display pegs for neck pieces. And a velvet chair to sit on while I buckle my shoes. Oh, I have the vision. This is the wardrobe of my dreams. Actually, it's more like a boutique. But without the bitch in the corner giving me attitude. The only bitch in that room will be me.

I don't want to gender type, but I don't think men have wardrobe fantasies. I don't think there's a big boofy bloke out there visioning a special display section of his wardrobe for his blue singlets and hi-vis vests. The only fantasy he's likely to have may involve a closet, but it won't be for putting things in, it will be for coming out of. This fabulously lit fantasy chamber that I dream of does not exist for a woman on my meagre budget. I have to be realistic. I must subsist on four shelves, and 2 metres of rack. I must learn to push down this yearning for a Barbie wardrobe, and put up with my lower middle class suburban Kath and Kim version. I don't actually sulk about it, but I reckon if I thought about it long enough I could.

It does seem like a trivial injustice when one considers there are probably places in the world where a family of five live in a wardrobe the size of mine. The amount of time I spend thinking about my wardrobe – how it could be better organised, more aesthetically pleasing or more opulent – is a reminder of a personality defect that I'd rather not admit. I'm shallow. I'm actually really a lot shallower than I'd care to admit. I only bought *Eat, Pray, Love* so people would think I'm deep. I think that's pretty shallow. Meaningless things mean a lot to me. Just last week I spent over an hour thinking about wallpapering the walk-in wardrobe and installing a chandelier so that while the space is small, it can still be grandiose. What a wardrobe wanker.

I guess my humble wardrobe keeps me honest. It also curbs my consumption. If I want something new, I have to throw something out. Although I did solve this riddle the other day. I bought something new and threw something of my husband's out. I have always struggled with letting go, but all I had to do was change my mindset and now it's a lot easier than you'd think!

THE BEEP TEST

Beep, beep, beep, beep, beep, beep, beep.

My fridge

*E*verything beeps. My toaster beeps. My phone beeps. The ATM at the bank beeps. The self-serve check-out at the supermarket beeps. My washing machine beeps, not just to let me know when it's finished but also when it's unbalanced. Why do I need a beep for that? This is a machine. Last time I checked, machines don't have needs and should be able to wait for my attention, rather than throwing annoying electronic tantrums. Sure, it's good to be aware that my washing machine is freaking out from the unsettling episode of having an unbalanced load – but must I drop everything right now to go and deal with it? Is it really a life and death situation worthy of beeping?

I have often thought that it might be handy for my loved ones if I had a similar beep setting so they knew the best time to approach me with stressful news. 'Don't tell Mum about failing the maths test, she's unbalanced today. Can't you hear how she's beeping?' Sometimes I wish I could resort to unrestrained beeping so someone else would come to my rescue and deal with the problem at hand. Actually, I have been beeping for years: my family call it 'whingeing', and thus far when it comes to results, it's exacted a perfect ZERO.

My clothes dryer beeps. My dishwasher beeps. My hair iron beeps. My fridge beeps. In fact the other day the fridge was beeping so loudly and insistently I was convinced it must have been reversing. Why does a fridge need to be so angry? Couldn't the manufacturers have programmed it to have a more soothing beep? Something slightly less anxiety producing? A purr perhaps. Or maybe a quiet sob. Fridges seem to be almost as difficult to please as children. My fridge was beeping because apparently it didn't like its internal setting. In fact, my fridge was pissed. It was unrelenting. That bastard of a thing beeped all night. I kept thinking that it would give up – that it must be have an internal reset that happens when the owner of the fridge refuses to respond.

I couldn't hold out. I got up at 2 am and spent 20 minutes trying to reset the internal setting back to something my fridge was comfortable with. It got me thinking, though. If a fridge is smart enough to complain about its internal setting, couldn't the person who created the computerised mechanism have included an automatic reset so it eventually shuts the fuck up? Or here's a tip, can't it revert to the previous setting? Can't they give the stupid fridge a memory? They've given it a beeping mechanism, it seems cruel to not allow it learning intelligence. I want to be able to leave the fridge alone to let the demanding thing sort itself out. That would be the fridge equivalent of controlled crying. Where after a tough night trying to break the fridge's spirit, you wander into the kitchen to find it curled up sleeping peacefully in the corner … and you look at it with a tear in your eye and think, 'I couldn't love that fridge more.' But no. My fridge is so codependent. It needs me. The worst thing about codependent appliances is that they are so bloody controlling. The fridge has these terrible panic attacks if things don't go how it likes. If I leave the door open while I'm cleaning for what the fridge considers too long, it will start emitting these frantic beeps.

My arch enemy at Fisher and Paykel clearly knows the exact timing and pitch for the most anxiety producing repetitive noise possible. It's like the fridge is in distress and is shouting at me, 'Help, help, help, help!' As if I have somehow caused the fridge harm by letting his cold air out. And yes, my fridge is a bloke. Anything that resistant to change would have to be a man. The other day I was standing by the sink with my hands halfway up a frozen chicken, shouting at the fridge, 'If you want your door closed that badly, do it your beeping self!' He kept beeping. No, I had to do it. Fucking typical. Then the beeps became more aggressive. Threatening. In fact I could have sworn that between every beep there was an abusive scream of, 'Fucking beech!' So I had to remove my hands from chicken. Wash hands. Close fridge. Beeping stopped. Then the chicken started. I didn't know frozen chickens could beep. Turned out it was not the chicken. It was the alarm on my iPhone telling me I had to go get the kids from the bus stop.

I visualised the children not being picked up by their mother. They are seated at the bus stop. Everyone else has been picked up except them. The children start beeping. Loudly, insistently. Then everyone in the street knows they haven't been collected by their bad, bad mother. Imagine having to walk home from the bus stop. Surely that must be reportable as child abuse!

So I got in the car and reversed down the driveway. It's a long way backwards so I don't wear my seatbelt. My car isn't happy about this. It starts beeping. Oh for crying out loud, I am 46 years old, can't I make my own safety decisions? This insistent nagging reminder to wear a seatbelt is like having my nanna in the car muttering, 'It isn't safe.' There have been many other times in my life where a beeping reminder would have been useful. Perhaps it would have saved me from harm. Like when I had unprotected sex. When the powers that be manage to invent a penis that starts beeping and renders itself useless unless a condom is rolled on, I will nominate them for a Nobel prize. But until then I'm not living my life ruled by beepers.

I'm not wearing a belt. I don't care what the car thinks. I don't care how much it insists. It's my decision. I am not anti-seatbelt. It's just that sometimes I don't want to tolerate the mindless beeping of my do-gooder car.

There are only two other instances when I don't wear a seatbelt: when I'm eight months pregnant, and when I have a fresh spray tan. I know it seems shallow but if I'm paying $40 for a nice job, then I don't want the silhouette of a seatbelt either.

Since when did we need appliances to beep? When did we need appliances to call us to order? Are we that stupid that we can't work out when our toast has popped, the dishwasher has finished its cycle or the fridge door is open? When did we no longer realise what was best for us? What happens when we live in a world where we start to trust the beep instead of ourselves?

How do we develop the skills to make good decisions, to save ourselves, to turn our shit off without the beep? No wonder we're all careering over the edge into the abyss of an Armageddon – because there was no beeping. Global warming, species extinction, extreme weather and the melting of the polar caps is not enough warning. Something should have started beeping! How were we to know that our resources were running out and we'd left the earth's fridge door open?

I question the philosophical implications of beep reliance and this intrinsic belief that we are fuckwits. And why, when you have the technology at your fingertips to install any sort of warning device, would you use a beep noise? Why not a bird call? A Barry Manilow track? A sermon by the pope?

Who out there thought that installing a noise pitched at peak irritation level thus allowing machines to have their own way was a good idea? Yes, I've seen the movie *Her* with Joaquin Phoenix and I can see what's coming. I've done enough personal growth workshops to know how to draw the line on toxic relationships and now, alongside controlling men, it looks like I have to include controlling appliances as well.

Beeping has this way of eroding the spirit. You can't argue with a beep. It's not rational. It doesn't allow you to compromise. You can't mediate and come to an arrangement like, 'Look, I can see you want me to close the door – so just give me five minutes to get my hands out of the chook and I'll be right there.' At which point the fridge says, 'Well, it's not what I wanted to start with, but I can see that is a better outcome than me having my door open all night so okay, I'll wait.' And then it stops beeping.

My kids came out the womb beeping at me. The only thing programed at a pitch more anxiety producing than a beep is a baby cry. Beeps just make you angry and uptight. Baby cries can break your heart. Eventually the human beep evolves into, 'Mum, mum, mum, mum.' And god knows there's no shut-off button for that. They just know there is a point where the 'Mum mum' will invade a woman on a cellular level and she'll stop anything she's doing and scream, 'WHAT?' But at least there's a chance of reasoning with a kid. 'Go away, Mummy's busy closing the fridge.'

You can't reason with a machine. They're bloody relentless. Once the car started beeping at me because I'd put my $500 designer handbag on the passenger seat. There is a certain etiquette in owning expensive handbags. They don't go on the floor. That's for dogs and shopping. I NEVER put that bag on the floor. It gets its own frickin' chair. I once made one of the kids stand on the bus just so my bag got a seat. It's more about preventing scuffing than it is about safety. But the car doesn't care about scuffing. It's all about safety. See, that's not smart. Technology isn't smarter than us after all. The car has decided the bag is so heavy it needs a seatbelt. It won't stop beeping at me. I yelled at the car, 'Its a handbag, you idiot.' In the end I got so sick of the noise I pulled over and did the seatbelt up.

I guess on the upside, while my car is an authoritarian dictator, at least my handbag was both unscuffed and safe from accidents. I don't know about you, but I am tired of devices telling me what to do. So I've started ignoring them. The other night the fire alarm was going ballistic, like totally mental. As with the kids, and the fridge, I refuse to respond to that kind of inappropriate and rude behaviour. I mean, it's 2 am. It's no time to be demanding a woman's attention. You have to set boundaries, otherwise the kids, and your appliances will run rings around you.

Yes, well, maybe there was a little fire. I guess I'll chalk that up as a 'learning consequence when trying to modify challenging behaviour.'

I might have lost a toaster, but I showed that flipping beeper who was boss. Oh, and I worked out why the fridge keeps beeping – it's broken. Oh, for Beep's sake!

THE PET PROJECT

A good dog deserves a good home.

Traditional proverb

I have always had pets. In fact, I don't remember a time in my life when there wasn't something small and furry giving me the fully dilated pupilled 'Feed Me Please!' stare. It's amazing how good you get at ignoring that. Long ago I developed a technique for delaying the feeding of pesky pets. I put them outside. In a way, having pets was like a warm-up for becoming a parent. Now when the kids start lumbering around the kitchen moaning, 'There's nothing to eat,' I lock them outside. It takes some practice, but eventually you can harden yourself to the starving faces pressed against the glass. As long as you can't hear them, your sanctuary is restored. You just have this rather grotesque visual. That's when you draw the blinds. It's an effective delay, although it does require a bit of post-begging Windex to remove the greasy fingers and saliva dribbles.

It's been said before, but there really is something magical about coming home to someone who is genuinely excited to see you. It's not like every time I come home my husband is jumping up and down licking my legs with the excitement of it all. The kids barely look up from their iPad, iPhone, iLife when I walk through the house. But the dog acts like I'm Kanye, and that's when I've only taken the rubbish out.

It never ceases to amaze me how much our little dog loves us. He really deserves a better family. A family more devoted to him. A family that dotes on him. A family that remembers they actually have a dog. I don't think the kids have touched him in about four years. Which is ironic because I do remember they were the ones asking, 'Can we have a dog? Can we have a dog? Can we have a dog?'

The other day my eldest daughter started up again: 'Can we have a dog? Can we have a dog? Can we have a dog?' Our dog, a Shih Tzu Maltese cross called Elvis, was sitting unnoticed at her feet. I said, 'But we have a dog.' She was clearly unprepared for this line of new pet purchase deflection. 'But I want a puppeeeeee.'

Oh god. A puppy. I don't like puppies. I know that's an unpopular statement. It's like saying, 'I don't like babies.' When you say that to people they look like you've slapped them and you know that on the way home in the car they're bitching about you. 'I can't believe Mandy, she doesn't like puppies! Who doesn't like puppies? She is such a witch.' Suddenly in my social circle I'm being hailed as Cruella De Ville.

When I say I don't like puppies it doesn't mean I don't walk past people in the street with puppies and say, 'Oh, isn't he gorgeous!' Then I give the puppy a pat and walk on. I have no desire whatsoever to take that tiny bag of yelping, shitting, pissing need home. I have five children of my own, and that's about as much yelping, shitting pissing need that one woman can handle in a lifetime.

My daughters, on the other hand, are afflicted with that adolescent-borne puppy love. They imagine the joy of cuddling that sweet little puppy. Having that tiny tongue lick their cheeks. Having people stop in the street gushing, 'Oh, what a gorgeous puppy!' And it's their puppy! They get the attention! They are the owners of the gorgeous puppy. Girls are dreamers, not realists. They don't for one moment imagine the vomit charging up their throat as they cup toilet paper around a steaming hot turd right in the middle of their new Country Road quilt cover. No, in their imaginations, cute little puppies don't crap. Or piss on their iPhone 6. Or chew the charger. And the GHD.

But that's what puppies do. Puppies, like babies, also cry when they don't get enough attention. I said to my daughter the other day, 'If you get a puppy you need to stay home with it. You can't go to work, or study or go out at night.' She looked at me with disbelief. The ongoing pet care regime hadn't occurred to her. You see, the wanting of puppies, the lust for cuteness, far outweighs the practical drudgery of good pet ownership. In her mind she was going to carry it around and cuddle it until she went away for the weekend with her boyfriend, or down to Melbourne, or overseas, and then I guess the puppy would end up with me. I don't think that's good for me, or for the puppy. As I said before, I don't like puppies.

Puppies are too much work. Sure I love my dog, but I love him now because he's a dog. I did not enjoy the puppy stage where he was just a ball of stupid shitting cuteness. It was exhausting. Neediness is not an attractive quality in anyone, and two years of freak outs every time you left the room did my head in. It's like living with a pathetic boyfriend. 'Where's she gone? Is she coming back? What if she never comes back? Where am I? I'm cold? I'm scared? Oh no, I just pissed myself again. I might chew this door.' And then it starts crying.

At least when you wake up to a crying baby in the night you have the option to breastfeed it. It's hard to cry with a tit in your mouth. I've proved this using both babies and men. The tit, however, is not a very effective silencer for dogs. And if you do resort to that, I can tell you, even the biggest animal lovers will start to talk.

I was so relieved when Elvis started behaving like a dog. He lost that eager-to-please desperation and replaced it with a kind of self-contained internalised desperation which I just have so much respect for.

The kids have no idea how much work it took to make that dog functional. When they were in bed sleeping, Mummy was up taking him for his five-kilometre walk each day. He spent most of his day hanging out with me. That house was right on a main road, poorly fenced and Elvis was a digger. I think he staged an escape from Alcatraz every two days. I'd find the hole and fill them with bricks. Then he'd find another spot to dig out and our game continued. I must have seen him run underneath a dozen cars and then come out the other side like nothing had happened. I was even considering renaming him Houdini. He could not be contained. So he slept in the house. I am not fond of 'inside' dogs. But we didn't have a choice. Unless he spent a significant amount of time 'inside' he'd end up like poor Daisy, our first and much less successful puppy. Any more pet death and I'd need to permanently enrol the kids in grief therapy.

I killed our first puppy. Not on purpose. By accident. Although the part of me that doesn't like puppies also suspects that had I not been such a hard arse, poor little Daisy would still be drinking from her dog bowl. Our first puppy died a horrible death because we'd decided to try her being an 'outside' dog. Before you judge me too harshly as a pet murderer, please realise that I hadn't owned a dog since I was ten. I actually had no idea about what it took to look after a puppy and help it become a fully rounded dog. It was like having babies all over again, where you have a cuddle and then put them down and think, 'What the fuck do I do now?'

Like with the kids I decided that it couldn't be that hard because people had been doing it forever. Ever since caveman bonded with his best friend, humans and dogs had hung out. It's not like they needed puppy bootcamp or to read books on dog training. Caveman got the dog thing sorted with a few grunts. And like a good cavewoman, I was keen to keep inside the cave for human habitation and outside the cave for dogs.

We made Daisy's bed in the outside laundry and as the fencing wasn't quite complete, we put her on a leash. A long leash so she could go for a run. I had no idea of all the leash-related injuries and dangers such a safety harness could apply to a young pup. I didn't even know there was such a thing as a harness. No, the leash was clipped to Daisy's collar.

I guess you must be able to tell where this is going. One morning, when Daisy was maybe only 14 weeks old, a sweet little bundle of black and white fluff, I opened the back door at 6.30 am to where I usually greeted her. It was strange that on this particular day that there was no movement. Must have slept late like us, I thought. I threw the back door open and then I saw it. Daisy's lead stretching from the laundry up the stairs. On the top step it had dropped off. The dear little puppy was dead. She'd hung herself on the leash I'd clipped to her so she wouldn't run off. I tried to stop the kids coming out before they saw her but it was too late, Sophia was at the door just as I cut her free. It was awful. Sophia was only nine at the time, and has always had this knack for saying something incredibly inappropriate. She couldn't have thought of anything to make me feel worse.

'Just like Uncle Michael.' The girls' uncle was Michael Hutchence, who was found hanged in his Sydney hotel room in 1997. His tragic suicide has cast a long shadow over the girls' paternal family, and I have always tried to protect them from the gossip and speculation that surrounded their uncle's death. Those kind of family stories are like deep scars, you certainly don't want to do anything to restart the bleeding. Like hang the puppy.

I cried for nearly a week. That's when I decided that I didn't like puppies. I couldn't get the image of Daisy's lifeless little body out of my head. Of course we dug the obligatory hole in the backyard and had an impromptu funeral. I tried to cheer the kids up with a painting of sunflowers for their bedroom called 'Sunflowers for Daisy'. I even planted a few on her tiny grave. It was all a bit macabre and not the first puppy experience I wanted for my kids. Wow, I had really fucked that one up.

The kids gave it a two-month breather before the chant started up again; 'Can we have a puppy can we have a puppy can we have a puppy?' And would you believe it? Just ten days before Christmas and I'm walking past the pet shop a few doors down from our house. And there's a puppy. An eight-week-old black fluffy little Elvis. He's adorable. Except for his overbite. But that made him kind of cuter because he was terminally ugly and terminally cute at the same time. And he was only $500. The kids had some Christmas money, I had guilt, and a plan to restore my children's faith in my ability to keep their pet alive. So I bought the puppy.

My husband couldn't really say no. I didn't actually ask him. After all, it was Christmas, and it was he who'd declared martial law on dogs being allowed in the house. So I knew he felt that it was partially his fault. He had a thing about animals in the house. His parents had had a labrador, a gorgeous large stinking blonde who created a pong in the house so powerful that when I was once eating roast lamb all I could smell was lab. I felt like I was eating Bouncer.

There is nothing better than a puppy for Christmas. Even when you don't like puppies. Thankfully, this little guy was tough. Where Daisy was very much of the submissive type of personality, Elivs was definitely dominant. I think to survive in our family you need to be dominant. There's no room in our pack for submissive types.

So that was how Elvis became an 'Inside Dog'.

Years on when I built a beautiful new home surrounded by red clay I took one look at the furry little fucker and said, 'Mate, I don't know how to break this to you, but you are going to become an Outside Dog.'

You can't do that with a cat. I tried to keep the cat out of the house but he just gave me one of his Big Ginger looks of, 'Go fuck yourself lady, I'm a cat, I'll go where I like. See this, I'm drinking in your shower. And in your toilet. Now I'm putting my toilet feet all over your nice clean kitchen bench. And see my tight little kitty cat arse, it's on the breadboard.'

As far as pets go, when I do a damages incurred audit on the cat and dog I have to say the cat comes up trumps when it comes to actual dollar for dollar destruction.

Dogs grow out of being chewers, and apart from the odd indiscretion, they're generally pretty easygoing. The dog doesn't want to piss you off. The dog wants you to look at him and say 'Good dog! Who's a good dog!'

The cat doesn't give a shit. In fact, I think our cat wrecks stuff just to show me the whole lock-me-outside-at-feeding-time-bitch is just my sad attempt to maintain a control I don't have in the first place. He will always win. Lollie (our 12-year-old desexed ginger furball) has destroyed one designer armchair, two couch settings, one leather dining room chair, and he's coughed up long orange sausage-shaped hair balls on nearly every surface in the house. He constantly walks mud through the house. Jumps on the couch with mud paws. Walks on my expensive quilt covers. When it comes to ruining sheet sets, he prefers Country Road and Linen House. He never seems to walk on anything I've bought from Target. Bloody snob. And if he notices I've washed the car, he'll jump on that and slide down the windscreen, just to make sure the job is complete! He's left a decapitated and subsequently decomposing rat on my bed as a 'welcome home' after a week away and I'd asked the neighbour to feed him. Occasionally if he gets locked in the house he'll drop a giant shit on the bath mat. Or the rug. Anything brown. Nothing like good poo camo to lure an unsuspecting toe right into the squishiness of it all. He's a maniac. Just the other day I came home to find him in the backyard taking on a 3-metre brown snake. The snake had reared up ready to strike, and there was Lollie all fluffed up ready to take him out. I thought I hated that cat, but then the prospect of losing him to a snake bite had me screaming and throwing rocks until the cat and the snake darted in opposite directions. Not understanding the imminent danger, I saw his backward glance of, 'Now the bitch is throwing rocks'. I'm nervous about his evil revenge plot. Terror Alert on the home front is currently set to High. That night I was so greatful to his furriness, I actually patted him and fed him without the two-hour lockout.

The dog sleeps on his little bed, chews up the odd stuffed toy and digs holes under trees to make a cosy bed. He's no match for the cat. Although he is capable of random and unexpected acts of sneakiness. Like the other day when John said, 'Nobody touch

these biscuits. These are the biscuits for a workshop I am running.'
John comes home, there's just crumbs in the packets and he gives
the kids some stick. 'I told you not to eat the biscuits!' They all
looked innocent, shocked that they could be so wrongly accused
of an offence they did not commit. Then Zoe says, 'That's weird,
I found crumbs in my bed.' And Sophia says, 'There were crumbs
all over my bedroom floor!' The biscuit detectives follow the trail
of crumbs to find the culprit lying on his back near his little
doggy bed surrounded by a halo of pink icing crumbs groaning
in pain because he has eaten sixteen biscuits. He's actually tried
to hide his offence by sneaking in the house and eating them in
Zoe's bed. That is so stupid and so funny none of us can be angry.
Dumb dog stuff like that just makes you love your dog more.

I was worried that Elvis wouldn't survive transitioning into
an Outside Dog. We didn't even have a fence. But at least we
weren't on a busy road. Would he feel rejected? Unloved? Would
he sit outside and cry to come in? I am happy to say none of that
happened. Elvis was in heaven. The dog who spent his life digging
out was now free. He didn't even seem to mind not coming inside.
John's office is downstairs and sometimes he sits at his master's
feet, or he'll sneak in to visit the girls. But he has several outside
beds tucked up close to the living areas and he's happy with that.
In fact, when it was storming I tried to bring him in and all he
did was stand at the door barking to get out. He's not a dog who
likes to be contained. He is, by nature, an outside dog. Free to
chase chickens, the neighbour's cat, rumble the sausage dog and
go for afternoon walks with his new mate Bruno, a Staffy who

lives up the road. It hasn't occurred to Elvis that Bruno could eat him in one bite. The idiot thinks he's an equal. Possibly even Bruno's superior. Classic small dog syndrome.

Sure, there are people out there who would think we are some sort of abomination in the pet owners' world. We don't allow the dog on the couch. The dog doesn't sleep on human beds. The dog has rules. It means the house doesn't stink and if anything is broken or damaged, we blame the cat. Small dogs are generally so indulged they end up with the Small Dog personality. Elvis is a Small Dog who gets treated like a Big Dog. Elvis, we realised, doesn't know he's a Small dog. Elvis is a Small Big Dog. He is king of the hill, and even though I complain about him and say I hate him and the cat, it's not true. They're very much part of the family.

Just don't tell them. Their constant need for my approval gives me the edge. It certainly doesn't work on the kids.

Maybe I should start keeping them outside too.

TOILET TALK

The worst job in the whole world must be recycling toilet paper.

Chuck Palahniuk, *Fight Club*

I have an unnatural attachment to my own toilet. It's the only place I can poo. When it comes to the 'throne' zone, I'm a one-loo woman. While some may applaud my lavatory based monogamy, I have to admit it is very limiting when I travel. This kind of defeats the purpose of having a relaxing 'get away'. Being constipated is not relaxing. It's awful.

A well-balanced person needs to be a poly-toileter. Someone able to take a dump any time, any where. Not me. I'm classic anal retentive. Any trip lasting longer than a week has me in extreme abdominal distress. It's a family trait. Clearly this is why no-one in our family ever travelled. They couldn't leave their potty.

You don't have to be a psychiatrist to deduce this kind of attachment to one's toilet is not normal. I am well aware of that. I am led to believe though, by the kind people at the laxative section in the pharmacy, that it's not uncommon. There are many weirdos just like me who have change-resistant bowels. Boring bowels. Insecure bowels. They are the bowels less travelled.

It's not a conscious thing. If I could will myself to 'Let it Go' in another toilet, then don't you think I would have done that already? I definitely can't poo at other people's houses. It feels like I'm being rude. 'Thanks for having me, and by the way, I just dropped a big turd in your loo.' I can't perform my ablutions if I can hear people chatting. Or drinking tea. Or eating. If I can hear them they can hear me. No, I need total quiet. Isolation. If I am to use a toilet that is not my own, it must be in another country. And there has to be a lock on the door. And something to read.

I don't understand the link between reading and pooing. Like books suddenly relax the large intestine. It makes me a bit worried about reading in a public setting. Like how do my bowels know if I'm in a toilet or in a plane? I gather it's pretty dark in there.

I find hotel rooms a bit challenging as well. I can't go if my husband is lying on the bed. A romantic evening goes a bit pear-shaped when you start to hear bottom music echoing in the bowl. Similarly I find the whole toilet in the ensuite a perplexing addition to the marital bedroom.

Why would I want to poo so close to where I sleep?

In the old days the toilet wasn't in the bedroom. Is our need for instant gratification so great that we can't even be bothered walking to the toilet anymore? No wonder we're all getting so fat. What's next? An actual bedpan? In the old days, there was one toilet, somewhere down a hallway. And before that people had to actually walk outside into the backyard! Talk about remote access.

While I am fine with the concept of the backyard toilet, I know that wouldn't be a solution for me. I'd be trading one anxiety for another. While my ensuite or in-house attempts at release are always governed by a fear of being discovered, my out-house toileting would be plagued with a fear of discovering. Snakes, rats, spiders … they are all the things that can take up residence in an insecure location if you squat for too long.

All this toilet talk has got me thinking about the actual toilet. Did you know there's actually an event called World Toilet Day? For those who like to celebrate special days, this is one to mark on your calendar. November 19 is hosted by the World Toilet Organisation and raises awareness for the 2.5 billion people in the world living without proper sanitation.

While the World Toilet Organisation (WTO) is a global not-for-profit organisation, you don't see Angelina Jolie or Victoria Beckham scrambling to the front of the pack to be a spokesperson for sanitation. While access to toilets are extraordinarily useful and good-health promoting, there's nothing really sexy about putting your face on a pisshouse. If I was a member of the WTO (I am seriously thinking about joining) I'd be petitioning famous comedians – after all, don't we make our bread and butter from toilet talk? In our house potty mouth isn't washed out with soap, it's praised and given chocolate.

While nobody can actually name the person who invented the first toilet, it happened around 3000 BC. Some genius got tired of digging a hole around the perimeter of their property and worked out that one hole dug once, was eminently more efficient than a new hole dug every time. It also saved one from the horror of an 'over dig' … when a new hole was dug on the site of a previous dig.

The Romans were pioneers of the public toilet. There were up to 144 communal lavatories available for anyone prepared to place their bum on a long bench. And to make it even more community minded, the Romans used a sponge on a stick for toilet paper and then rinsed it off and left it for the next person! While they had the 'sewage' collection concept down, I don't think they had the 'privacy' or 'hygienic' part nailed. For the most part I think the average Roman just threw their waste onto the street.

A prelude to our modern-day defecator was the garderobe. This was a medieval English invention – it operated along the same lines as old railway trains used to – the room protruded over a moat and there was a tiny opening in the floor out of which all the royal arseholes did their business. The poop would fall into the moat. How romantic … a castle, surrounded by shit. Now I know why no-one ever crossed the moat to attack the castle!

It's kind of sad how our technologies haven't evolved that much. A lot of cities still send their shit out to sea in the vain hope that the ocean has a magical poo-disappearing power. It does disappear. Out to sea. But the sea always leads to a seashore somewhere. They didn't call them Bondi cigars for nothing.

The first flushing toilet was invented by Thomas Crapper. I think. I don't care if it's wrong, I just love the evolution of his last name. I love the way language does that. Takes someone's last name and attributes it to an invention, thereby making that particular last name a source of humiliation, embarrassment and playground bullying. Just think if a Kardashian had invented it, we'd be shitting in the Kardashian, rather than just watching the shit.

I still remember using an outhouse. An old aunt of mine had one at her house, and living in country Australia in the early 1970s you'd occasionally come across the odd house that still enjoyed the comforts of a wooden box. In a way it's ironic how the toilet that got 'flushed' out by the invention of the in-house cistern just push a button and whoosh that nasty poo is gone, is now making a comeback in the form of a modern day composting toilet.

The outhouse was terrifying. For a start, it smelt. It smelt like shit. I guess it makes sense that toilets smell, it discourages staying in them too long. But I was used to living in a house that flushed away the pong. I was part of a new generation of humans unaccustomed to the sanitary horror of what human habitation actually smells like. If you've ever kept a pet mouse you'll know what I'm talking about. All the mouse wee and poop in a confined space gives off a particularly rancid and pungent odour. Humans aren't really any different. We've just learnt to use water.

So being a flusher and confronted with a small shack housing a wooden box containing a tin full of the family ablutions was a little traumatising. You might say that I never forgot those trips to Great Aunt Harriet's. I was literally shit scared – and wouldn't be surprised if this wasn't the exact point in time when my traveller's bowel first started.

There was never a light in the outhouse. Just a box of matches, a roll of loo paper and a bucket of sawdust containing a cup that I was certain matched the cup Aunt Harriet served my milk in last night. Sawdust, for those who are unfamiliar with the ways of the outhouse, replaced water. You basically buried your shit. That half cup of sawdust you threw on top was charged with the duty of hiding your business and damping down the smell. It did nothing to alleviate my suspicion that I was using the human version of a kitty litter tray.

As a child I was terrified I would fall into the hole. It was easy to believe in monsters when the backyard contained a place where monsters were made. It was always so dark in there. I guess the darkness had a purpose. Full incandescent lighting would have revealed a myriad of horrors – like redback spiders, brown snakes and paedophiles who lurked in the dark corners. You also didn't want to see inside the hole. You didn't want to see the inner workings of who had gone before you – but if it was the end of the week before the night soilman who had the delightful job of 'collecting' aforementioned shit cans, or Dad who had some sort of shit-pit burial ground in the backyard – you generally did. Those same Dads always seemed to have unexplained good fortune with the productivity of their vegie patches. In fact, I've never seen pumpkins so big.

I do like my flushing toilet. This goes against my inner desire to be a proper environmentalist. So does my disregard for recycled toilet paper. No, when it comes to the land of loo I am guilty of being another planetary pillage. Stealing my children's children's children's children's future, one poo at a time.

My friends have a pit toilet. I remember being asked over to view their new country property and being struck speechless at the inclusion of this chamber of horror. The house was lovely, but the toilet? It filled me with unspeakable fear. While everyone gathered around congratulating the happy couple on what a jolly good idea the pit toilet was and how this was the way of the future, I fell silent. How could I tell my friends their ideologically sound toilet frightened me? More than the outhouse of my childhood. At least if you fell in that you only fell in a tin. No, a pit toilet has a drop. Up to 3 or 4 metres straight down into the chasm of darkness. Staring down that black hole was like staring into my own soul. I had no idea what was going to jump out. It was such a relief to realise that my arse was of a sufficient size that it was a physical impossibility for me to fall in. However, the same could not be said for a small child.

Pit toilets provide significant risk for small children. I have no idea how many fall in each year, but there has to be at least a couple. I mean, when faced with a stinking black hole leading to a cess pit, what child doesn't wonder if this mightn't be some sort of portal to Narnia, had a little peek and then found themselves literally 'in the shit'?

I think pit toilets need pool fencing. Or at least a minimum arse-size requirement for users to ensure toileting safety. There's a lot of horrible ways to die, and if you can take 'death by drowning in shit' off the list, then you've done something positive for humanity. Incidentally, I don't know of any kids who've died from drowning in a flushable toilet. They may have got a bit sick from drinking the toilet water or licking the seat, but apart from that, the set-up is generally pretty safe.

I think we all take hygiene for granted. Things never used to be as clean as they are now. Until Dr Dettol and Mr Sheen turned up, we pretty well lived in filth. Toilets were disgusting places kept in the backyard so they didn't stink out the house. I know it's environmentally wrong, but how good is a gleaming white porcelain bowl? Perfectly clean! Glossy! Glowing with bleached lemony Toilet Duck goodness. When you look at a toilet, it's hard to believe it's not a salad bowl. I have serving platters that are not as impressively shiny and clean. Who hasn't worshipped the S-bend after a big night out has reduced them to a crawling mess on the bathroom floor, hugging the toilet for support? I once had a stomach infection that was so bad I slept on the tiles with my head on the seat. You wouldn't do that in a composting toilet. If you did I guess you'd have an answer for why you had birdcage mouth the next day: sawdust.

For all this advancement in home-based sanitation, it's amazing how good it is to go back to our caveman or cavewoman days and have an outside wee. Blokes do this all the time. In fact, they've got the perfect equipment. Why, they can have a chat, a beer and a wee all without actually having to stop turning the snags on the barbie. For us girls, the outside wee usually only happens when we're camping, or after a few wines. The lady squat takes considerable core strength, and involves leveraging one's arse away from one's ankle panties, ensuring that one is pissing slightly on the incline as opposed to the decline, so that feet, panties and the hem of one's frock doesn't become urine soaked. It's really a great way to feel part of nature. And its good for the lawn. Of course, if like me you live in suburbia, I might suggest you finish your fencing before you embark on a campaign of free wee.

Maybe this is the perfect therapy for anally retentive people like me. Maybe if I do this I can conquer my bathroom block. Maybe I can go on holidays longer than a week! Oh, imagine the freedom! No longer forcing myself to read the *Desiderata* over and over, choking down the gel shakes of psyllium husks and prune chasers! No longer having to worry about the state of people's toilets, or where they are in the house. No more.

A new woman.

A woman who can Free Poo.

LOVE THY NEIGHBOURS

You can change friends but not neighbours.

Atal Bihari Vajpayee (Indian statesman)

When Mark, one of Jesus's disciples, wrote 'Love your neighbour as yourself. There is no commandment greater than these,' he wasn't kidding. If you don't have a 'good' relationship with the people who live next door than it doesn't matter how much you perfect your paradise, you're living next door to hell. Nothing burns hotter than the flames of hate and resentment and, for some people, nothing stokes those flames higher than a misplaced bin or unmowed lawn. I don't know about you but I can't relax if I know the people who live next door are plotting my demise.

And it happens. A lot more than it should. Not to me necessarily but to lots of people living next door to people who they have decided to make their enemy. One awful story that came out of the UK was about a woman who torched the flat of her neighbour and killed five people, including a 15-month-old baby boy, a 2-year-old and a 4-year-old. And what was the impetus for such a murderous rage? A pram left in the hallway. How does the mild annoyance of a misplaced pram justify murder? Thinking back to when the kids were small I'm relieved I never lived in an apartment because I'm exactly the kind of woman who would have left her pram in the hall.

Small things send some people psycho. I have a theory about intolerant angry people like this and it's basically that they wait for stuff to happen so they can use it as 'cover' for their deeper hatred of humanity. When you've got a hair trigger you are just hoping someone does something 'wrong' so you can be 'right' and therefore justify losing your shit. These are very often the same people who'll blow a gasket if you accidentally cut them off in traffic or take their parking spot.

I have friends who live next door to a bloke who we will call Kevin. Kevin is a very neat, quietly furious man who spends his days looking for the fault in humanity. I'm not talking philosophical faults – nothing actually that impressive. No, Kevin is focused on my friends' neigbourly failings. If they put their bin anywhere remotely near the front of their property on rubbish collection day, Kevin will leave an abusive note on the bin and move it to the middle of the road, away from his property. Kevin is a neat freak. He has a well-known but seldom identified mental health issue that I like to call OCLD. Obsessive Compulsive Lawn Disorder.

Basically, people with OCLD believe that if they lose control of their lawn, they'll lose control of themselves. The lawn must be perfect. At all times. Edges are trimmed to perfection. Rogue grasses or dandelions are weeded. Lawn grubs poisoned. Lawn is mowed and mowed and mowed. You've seen these lawns. I've never owned one personally because I don't have OCLD. These are incredible lawns. The kind that make you think 'Man, I could take off all my clothes and roll naked on that lawn', it looks so soft and spongey. It's inviting. But people with perfect lawns don't want anyone touching them. They are for show. You never EVER see anyone doing anything on their perfect patch.

Kevin doesn't like the way his grass touches other peoples' and the way their grass grows in clumps, and is uneven, brown, bindi-ridden and, worst of all, long! Kevin leaves notes about the grass. Kevin doesn't like people parking out the front of his house. Kevin doesn't like untrimmed hedges or leaves daring to droop on his side of the fence. Kevin doesn't like most things. He particularly dislikes joy. Kevin is a cunt. And living next to him must take the compassion of a Buddha. After twenty years of living next door to Malice, my friends have decided that the simplest approach is to find Kevin amusing. Their refusal to be reactive and the fact that they are very often pleasant to a man who bears them nothing but ill will means Kevin never gets the satisfaction of an all-out war. Which is what Kevin clearly wants. It's hard to have a neighbour war when you live next door to the United Nations.

Getting upset about lawn clippings, sprinklers, kids laughing, people talking or a bit of music is stupid. It's the stuff of life. Humans infringe on other humans all the time, and in the give and take of the normal human traffic flow there will be times when we all need someone nearby to cut us a little slack.

My dog Elvis has a habit of barking at 5.30 am when the local ballooning company takes its patrons on a leisurely sunrise ride. The quiet of the dawn is permeated only by the whoosh of the helium 20 metres above our roof and my small dog who has decided we are facing attack by air. It's embarrassing. I know everyone in the neighbourhood is lying in bed cursing my dog. Which means by association they are cursing me for not having control of my mutt. In fact I have heard the odd yell of 'Fucking shut up!' emanating from the street. I don't know whether they are yelling at me for screaming 'ELVIS!' or Elvis for actually barking.

Fortunately no-one in my neighbourhood has got pissed off enough to either confront me or ring the ranger. I appreciate that and sincerely hope that after my repeated calls to the balloon company they will let me know in advance if we are to expect a dawn attack by air so I can gag my little protector.

When it comes to being a bad neighbour, the trifles of lawn clippings and leaf blowers are small fry. A truly bad neighbour is a serious fucking problem. And when I say bad, I mean living next door to a crack house. You can't deal drugs discreetly. Whether they want to let on or not, it doesn't matter. Everyone knows. Unless you are such an idiot that you think people really do pop over next door for multiple short visits because your neighbour makes an excellent cuppa. He makes an excellent cup of crack. Or heroin. Or pot. You can usually tell the pot house because it stinks of weed and there's reggae playing and while people turn up to score, they seldom go home under four hours. Generally because they're too stoned.

Drug lords make lousy neighbours. And if you hassle them about their untrimmed hedge you are likely to wake up to a room full of bikers assisting you to trim yours.

The party house is also a disaster. Doof music in the morning is enough to put your neighbours on blood pressure tablets. In fact, doof music at any time makes me feel a bit 'strokey.' Sometimes it can be harder living next door to a party house than the local drop-in drug depot. At least drug barons might consider keeping the lawn neat – after all they don't want anyone to know they're drug barons. But party house is full on anarchy that will eventually spill onto the street in the form of mountains of rubbish and drunken domestics. At some point at the party house someone is going to come undone and you will wake up at 3 am to a drunken fight between two blokes in their undies screaming, 'I'm gonna fucking kill you.' An hour later they'll be having a cuddle sobbing, 'I love youse mate. I didn't mean ta take ya lighter.'

A girlfriend of mine had the worst sort of neighbour. She had the sexual predator. At 17 this bloke had developed an obsession with the women in his neighbourhood and was breaking into their houses and taking their stuff. One woman woke to find him in bed with her. My friend had a feeling she was always being watched. She became especially unnerved when gardening one day to find clearly dug out trenches in the bushes where the dirty little perve had been getting his fill. Dirty little perve was eventually arrested.

I have been lucky enough to have mostly positive neighbourly experiences. I can easily pop next door for a cup of sugar, although in this organic whole food country, people tend to pop over with requests like, 'I was making a vegan bake and I realised I'd run out of quinoa!' And you answer, 'Oh no problems – do you want red or white?'

Good neighbours help each other out. I don't just have a spare key under the mat; I also have one next door at the neighbour's house. When we go away they feed our cat and water our garden. We look after each other's children. We sometimes throw sausages on the barbie and a few of the neighbours wander over. I feel like I'm living in the 50s. It's wonderful. I'm aware that most people these days may go a decade without ever knowing someone's name, let alone having them over for a snag.

Good neighbours also know how to give each other space. There's nothing worse than the needy neighbour who won't go home. The one who has popped over to return something they borrowed only to stay for dinner. Every night. On leaving they borrow something else. And you give it to them because you think they'll leave. And they do, but it's their ticket back tomorrow!

Dealing with neighbours is very much the realm of the poor. It seems the more socioeconomic privileges you have the more choice you have about where you live, who you live with and how close you live to them. As soon as some people make a lot of money, the first thing they do is buy a massive house on a huge property with a giant kickarse fence, electric gates and security monitoring. There ain't no popping over the fence for sugar in those neighbourhoods, unless by sugar you are meaning 'sex', which I'm lead to believe happens more than one would imagine.

John-Paul Satre once said that 'Hell is other people'. I don't know about that. I reckon hell might be being the sort of person who doesn't know how to get along with other people.

But then I would say that because I don't have a fence. Or a gate.

And I'm the woman who's one cup short.

FINDING HOME

There's no place like home.

Dorothy, *The Wizard of Oz*

When I was a kid I used to stare out my bedroom window, framed by the pale pink nylon curtain, and imagine the life I would live when I was grown up. I would not live in this shitty little country town. No way. I was destined for something far grander. I could feel it in my bones. My life was going to be exciting. And meaningful. And somewhere fucking else. I was going to live in the city. Somewhere like New York, or Paris. Or Toowoomba. Somewhere with traffic lights. And coffee. Somewhere where life was exciting. Not the TS Eliot regulation coffee spoon joy allocation metered out in regional Australia. I wanted my joy by the bucket full.

The life I envisaged starred a tall blonde with a slash of red lipstick decked out in a designer business suit jostling her fellow pedestrians as she raced to her audition or meeting or bikini wax. Of course, none of this ever came to be. It was a girlish fantasy. Life has a way of creating its own ironies. I ended up living in the country. And surprise, surprise, I love it.

It's me. I have faced the thing I spent my whole life running from. I am a country girl. And there's nothing wrong with that. The world needs country girls.

In my mind it's not really the country. It's far too crackpot for that. I live in Mullumbimby – famed for its rich dairy country, its magic mushrooms and its bush weed. Mullumbimby is just fifteen minutes north west from Byron Bay, nestled in the heart of the rainbow region, a curious mix of red necks, green necks, no necks and long necks. Counter culture came to the region in the 1970s, and the shoe-free, wild-bearded, pot-smoking, full-moon party dancing, hands-on healing Centrelink-dependent hippies have claimed this place as home ever since. Except now they tend to wear shoes and own property, eat meat but not gluten, and have traded their Indian names for their original Aussie ones because it all became far too common.

Mullumbimby is a curious mix of people. It's part of the town's mystique – this melting pot of conflicting ideologies, belief systems, conspiracy theories and food intolerances. Mullumbimby is the most unimmunised town in Australia. Almost 50 per cent of our population have decided that vaccines are some sort of super plot by Big Pharma to make our kids autistic and opted for a more 'natural' approach. That generally means giving the kids a homeopathic remedy or two and a good bacteria-filled lick on the cheek before they head out in the world. For a town that regards bureaucracies with such disdain, I find it amusing that it then imbues the same cretins with the ability to enact massive, well coordinated attacks on social order. I don't buy in. I immunise my children. Eat meat. And bread. And as far as I can tell, we're all doing okay. I just don't broadcast it. I don't want my children to be stigmatised at school as 'those weird meat-eating, gluten-loving immunisers'.

It's the defining principle of Mullumbimby: no-one ever lets the facts get in the way of formulating an opinion. It's something that annoys me, but at the same time I kind of like the ethos of being part of a community that thinks, lives and breathes outside the box. We are a community deeply suspicious of institutions. We don't want our children's creativity to be shut down by the system, so we send them to Steiner school with a lunchbox full of nori rolls and dried fruit to learn how to dance and do felting.

In an area with 30 000 residents, it's no surprise we have two Steiner schools that run from kindgergarten to high school. It's part of the grand plan to breed another generation that not only thinks outside the box, but are capable of inventing non box-like structures made entirely of organic substances.

I'm not that alternative. This is a terrible admission, but I hate chanting. People here love chanting. But it gives me anxiety. I find it annoying. I think it sounds like a bunch of blokes trying to cough up some phlegm. I went to see the Gyoto monks once and I was profoundly unmoved by the awful guttural throat song or the sand mandala. I remember thinking to myself, 'These blokes are taking the piss.'

I also don't have a moon calendar on the toilet door. I have a compost bin but I don't use it properly. It's just for show when my sustainable-living environmentalist friends pop over for peppermint tea. I eat sugar. I can't even pronounce quinoa, and I don't have a clue how to use it in a salad. I bought a bag of it last year and ended up using it in the kitty litter tray. I don't go to yoga. I find yoga boring. It's too slow. And you can't win at yoga. If they made yoga a contact sport I'd be into it. I don't meditate. That's for people with nothing to do except achieve enlightenment by making 'nothing' more important than it should be. I drink cow's milk. And I eat wheat. I watch television. I don't do liver detoxes. I actually prefer a bit of casual toxing. And I'm not remotely interested in tantric sex. Don't get me wrong, I love sex, it's just that I don't have time for three-hour long pleasuring sessions. I like to make love, have a quick cuddle then pop back on the computer to see if I can't nab the last bid on that handbag on eBay.

One day I realised what all these people from such disparate groups in Mullumbimby had in common. We are all black sheep. People that don't quite fit. I live in a town full of square pegs. Nobody asks too many questions here about what you do or where you come from. People kind of assume you'll tell them if you want to. Or not. They also assume that maybe you do nothing and don't want to embarrass you so they don't even ask. The only thing you get judged harshly for in Mullumbimby is being judgemental.

This is a strange place. I certainly never meant to live here or had any intention of making it my home. It's ostensibly a country town with an extraordinary number of coffee shops. At present we have seven excellent coffee shops in a town of 4000 people.

Most country towns this size are lucky to have one. It's clear that a good many of us have a little more leisure time than the rest of Australia. But man are we buzzed.

At one of my favourite coffee shops I came across a section in the menu that reminded me that my town was like no other. This particular establishment is built under a giant tree with fabulous large and sprawling gardens with eclectic and funky table settings scattered throughout. It's truly a beautiful place. On the back of the menu on the last page in size 48 font was the request, 'Please Don't Let Your Children Poo in the Garden'. They would have only put that in the menu if it happened more than once. I don't think I've ever been to a café anywhere else where someone's kid has taken a dump in a pot plant. Unfortunately, I don't know if that statement had any affect on the clientele, because the personality of the average punter is generally characterised by an unwillingness and, in some cases an actual inability, to take direction. The kids and I did a poo in the garden right there and then. You can't tell us what to do.

The thing about finding home is that you have to let it find you. I remember this awful feeling I had for years of never really knowing where I belonged. Who did I belong to? Where was the place and the people with whom I was going to build my life? Where was my home?

For some people this sense of home actually comes in movement. It's the gypsy like flow from place to place where they feel the strongest sense of community. But not me. I felt like there had to be an actual place for me. I moved to Byron Bay by accident twenty-five years ago. I only came because a boyfriend begged me to. We lived across the road from the beach. Every day I went swimming and lay in the sand. I was bored shitless. Paradise can really wear you down. It was nothing more than a prolonged holiday. One of those detours you take off your life path before you resume the main game. After six months the relationship was over. I was lost. I was working as a waitress in this surfie hippie outpost with barely a cent or a friend to my name. I had fallen off the grid and had no idea how to scramble back on.

I remember coming back from a weekend in Sydney on the bus. I'd gone south for the week to see whether I wanted to move to Sydney and I'd basically decided that it was going to be my next move. I was completely confused, but I suspected that Sydney was the place where I would have my life and find the girl I was supposed to be.

Then it happened. From the minute I got on the bus I started crying. Not just little tears, but proper big tears. By Newcastle I had sobbed my body weight in water. But it didn't stop. I wondered why life was so hard and lonely and where were my people? Where was my place? Maybe I didn't belong anywhere, except to the night on a bus. I stared into the dark as I wept. No-one sat next to me. No-one even asked if I was okay. Maybe this happened a lot. Maybe I was having a garden variety Greyhound bus breakdown.

Thirteen hours of grief interrupted only by a sausage roll at Taree and a potato scallop at the Big Prawn. I cried all the way to Byron Bay. It was like some sort of salt-based rite of passage. Partly I was crying because I was too poor to fly, but mostly because I didn't know who I was or where I belonged. I was lost, without a clue in the world about how I would find my way home. You can't go home when you don't have one. I was tired of looking. I'd given up. And now I just felt sorry for myself. I guess you could say I threw a thirteen-hour tantrum.

It was early when the bus dropped me in Byron. Maybe 7 am tops. I walked to the beach for some ocean therapy. After a thirteen-hour cry my face was swollen. It wasn't pretty. My eyes were puffed up like I'd been punched in the head. I felt like a complete dickhead. I was that girl in the crowd that you pretended not to look at but once she's passed you, you mutter, what the hell has happened to her?

People would assume a fight with a boyfriend, a death in the family, cancer. But no, nothing that concrete, just a loss of a sense of self.

I sat in the sand. It was a blazing mid-spring morning – the water was crystal blue and winking in the sunshine. The sand was white and clean. There was a soft breeze tickling my skin. As life would have it, I had stumbled in on the only kite-flying day Byron has ever had. (It's now a regular event in nearby Brunswick Heads.) Soaring in the sky were hundreds of vibrant kites and attached to the strings were people. Old people, young people, hippy people, straight people, surfie people, beautiful people, ugly people, ordinary people. People that I lived alongside but had never met. Or even noticed before.

That day on the beach I had the most overwhelming sense of home, that somewhere above me, unseen, was a string that connected me to these people and to this place. It was that simple. One sunny morning on the beach, a spiritual orphan found home.

It wasn't logical; it wasn't rational. For gods sake I was single, I was childless, I was young and I was ambitious for a career in the arts. Why would I live in a place associated with renegades and dropouts? Waitressing was basically the only job on offer. But I didn't care. Stopping was better than running. In a way I had been born running. And here finally, I allowed a place to still me. I could almost understand the thing indigenous people talk about when they say the land sings to them. It was like that. Wordless and profound and grounding. I became a different person sitting there. I felt like I was home.

Of course I've tried to leave. As much as I loved my home in Byron over the years I kept thinking that I was missing out. That there was a life somewhere else I was supposed to be living. There was a stint when I grabbed the kids and lived for eighteen months in Sydney. I hated it. I felt like I was withering. I am a country girl with a nature as expansive as my arse. As much as I loved the city, when I actually lived there I could never play the social game of not noticing or talking to other people who happened to be standing next to me. I am a talker. I would see someone's baby and coo, 'Wow she's gorgeous!' And then the parents would look at me like I'd asked, 'Could I have a bite?' I felt like I was living with zombies. I like to talk to strangers all the time. But in

Sydney people didn't know what to do, or to say, so instead they regarded me with suspicion and withdrew, giving me the 'Fuck off, crazy lady,' vibe. By the end I was the one patting my seat on the train encouraging crazy people to sit next to me. At least they were open for a chat, even if it was about the government spraying us with chemicals as a form of mind control. You know it's time to leave when the crazy people won't sit next to you.

So I moved back north and accepted that an ordinary life wasn't so bad. I could no longer afford to live in Byron as real estate had rocketed in response to the growing populations of groovers holidaying and moving here. Ironically, the same groovers that had eyed me with suspicion in Sydney now stopped me in the supermarket to ask advice on the best place to eat. I wasn't interested. I moved to Mullumbimby.

What I love most about Mullum, the affectionate shortening of its name, is the country town Sundays. It's the day when cafes and shops close. It's like the town is napping. It's my favourite day. For all its bustling weekly social activity, from Saturday lunch time to Monday morning, the place is asleep. You could cartwheel naked up the street and only be noticed by a passing dog. If you did the same on a weekday you'd be mistaken for a busker and make $20.

On Sunday mornings, if we aren't in the mood for the gruelling six-minute drive to the beach at Brunswick Heads, John and I opt for coffee and breakfast at the local swimming pool. There is something very country town about the country town pool. It's a meeting place where adults and children come together in their togs. I used to do it when I was a kid. In our economically aspirational society, more people have pools at home, so less people go to the local pool to share bacteria with their community. I think they are missing out. There is something special about Sunday at the swimming pool. Of course, I still want my own pool. I just appreciate this while I don't have one.

I drink coffee. John reads the paper. Ivy swims. Over the course of two hours we'll swim and sit and chat to the people who also wander in for their Sunday swim. These aren't 'friends' per se, but people we know from school, or a café, or just from our visits to the pool. I love that sense of community. It's randomness. I haven't organised to meet anyone. I haven't had to clean the kitchen because guests are coming over. I'm in a public place mingling with my community. It's like being wrapped in a warm blanket – sometimes it might get a bit stifling, but generally it's pretty wonderful.

And after all my years of hoping for a life, a career and a home so much grander and more impressive than the one I already have, I am reminded that what I do have is pretty bloody good. It only takes a Sunday at the pool to remind me, that home isn't just two minutes down the road, that it is in that quiet place of contentment inside me.

Welcome home.